Shame of the Vampire King

VAMPIRE KINGS
BOOK TWO

RHIANNON FUTCH

Ebook ISBN: **978-1-955749-06-0**

Print ISBN: 978-1-955749-21-3

Cover by sunsetrosebooks.com

Editing by V. Editing Services

Contents

One

Malic

Epaphras has already warned me there is a woman in the castle that I will need to deal with. What is Knox thinking? Why would he have one of those crown seeking twats hanging about in the castle? This is what comes from all that fucking of the humans he does. My brothers all think that I have no idea what they do while they are out roaming the world, but they would be dead wrong. I know where they are and who they are with at all times. Just because we need our time apart does not mean my job as a protector is over.

My failure to protect them did not absolve me from the job, and being apart certainly won't do it. Epaphras' warning convinced me to return early without telling anyone. I want to surprise everyone with my return, most especially this Valdís. However, since no one is expecting me, I have to dock the boat alone. No great hardship, just a little more focus.

Once I have my ship moored, I head directly for the garage nearby. There is a strange scent in the garage, faint but still present. It is the best thing I have ever smelled. What is that? Shrugging it off, I get on one of the bikes. I hate trying to squeeze myself into the cars. They are built for smaller people than I. Roaring off through the tunnels; I wonder just what state will the castle be in?

Knox has always been the most kind of us all. And the most soft-hearted. One good sob story and he would give her half the castle. I was soft once, and it cost me my brothers. It won't happen again. That smell is there again as I get to the other end of the tunnel. It is much stronger here, more distracting. Focus Malic, no distractions.

My appearance surprises the guards as I step off the elevator. They were in defensive positions, though, so I smile at them. "Excellent work. Did you notify anyone that I am here?"

"Yes, we followed protocol. I need to inform them that you are not a threat before half the guard is dispatched this way."

"Go ahead, but have them keep it quiet that I am here. I want to surprise my brother."

"As you wish, sire."

He turns and speaks into his comm device while I tell the other guard, "Report. What has happened recently? Why is there a woman in the castle?"

The guard tells me how this woman arrived at the

castle one day wanting to petition. Ever since she arrived, people from outside the castle have been trying to kill or kidnap her and the castle itself has suffered two explosions. He also informs me of the additional security measures installed on the outer walls and the recent kidnapping.

"Thank you. Do you smell that?" I can smell that scent on the breeze. It is the best scent I have ever smelled. My instincts want me to follow that scent to its source and devour it. I won't, but I will find out where it comes from. After I see my brother.

The guard looks at me like I have grown a second head as he tells me, "No, sire. I only smell the regular smells. Perhaps the castle smells different because you have been away so long?"

"Yes, that must be it. Thank you." I leave him and head into the castle, where the scent is so much stronger. Maybe it is just the way the castle smells now?

As I stride through the halls, Epaphras stops and stares at me from a crossing of halls, "Sire, you weren't due for days yet! Your room isn't ready. Why would you not give me a warning? Oh! You kings just do as you please, no regard for us working folk!"

I laugh, "I'm sorry Epaphras. I wanted to surprise my brother and catch him before he leaves."

"Well, your room isn't ready yet. It won't be until tonight. The only room currently ready is the guest room that was so recently blown up and repaired. And your brother isn't planning to leave anytime soon. I could have told you that if you had let me know, you were coming early."

Not leaving? "What do you mean, my brother isn't leaving?"

"Exactly what I said. He is staying. He has been waiting for your arrival. Did you injure your brain on the way in?"

The scent gets stronger and I close my eyes briefly, "Do you smell that Epaphras?"

"Smell what? What is it with you all and the smells lately? Are you sick? Can you lot get sick?"

"I'm not the only one that smells something?"

He scowls at me. "No, your brother and Valdís both smell something lately that I can't seem to detect. I think you are all nuts. If you don't need anything, sire, I will be off to have your room aired and cleaned."

I can't help but laugh as he stomps off. I call after him, "Where is my brother?"

"In his office!"

Shaking my head, I turn the opposite direction he is heading and start for my brother's office. I don't bother with knocking when I get to the door. I just open it and step in. He looks up from the paperwork he is handling, and for just a fleeting second, I swear I saw fear in his eyes. What would he have to fear from me? Unless the fear isn't for himself, but the little twat residing somewhere in the castle. "Hello brother. Tell me what has been happening in my absence."

He sighs. "I suppose you do need to hear it all."

I sit opposite him. "Before you start, what is the scent that is throughout the castle?"

"Smells like everything good in the world? Like you might die if you can't find it?" His description is so accurate I am a little afraid, but I nod and he says, "That is Valdís."

"You could just tell me what it is, absolutely ridiculous to attribute something that smells that good to a bitch that is here to use us."

Knox growls at me. Of all the shit, the motherfucker growled at me before he says, "Malic, I need you to hold your tongue until you meet her or I am going to rip it out again."

He is so serious. What has this bitch done to him? While I am not afraid of Knox, I humor him. "Fine. I will withhold judgment for now."

Knox tells me about the things that have been going on since the day that this Valdís appeared at the door seeking the right to petition. His telling of the tale is more thorough than the guard. Her mother is seeking to strip her of her inheritance? Her father's best friend wants to force her to marry his son and went so far as to kidnap her? What the fuck? Why? I know the holding the family has. It is nice but nothing that special.

"Knox, why? What is so special about her that these people that should care for her are trying to eliminate her as a threat one way or another?"

Knox looks away, toward our wing of the castle. "The room accepted her Malic."

He could have ripped my tongue out and it would have hurt less. "Don't fuck with me Knox, there is no way she has appeared after all this time. Not after we all finally gave up."

"I didn't want to believe it either, brother. There were other signs, the scent of her, for one. Then she was kidnapped by Ingemar's people and I couldn't focus. Finding her took hours longer than it should have, solely because I was too distraught to see the obvious culprits. Once I did, we recovered her quickly. I haven't quite decided what his punishment will be. Perhaps you would like to help make the decision?"

"Well, that is appealing. I think I will take you up on that. But first, I want to question her."

His eyes narrow as he tells me, "Maybe meet her and set up a time for questions later? Keeping in mind that she is not on trial."

"I will try. Let's get this over with."

He sends for Epaphras, who likely knows where everyone in the castle is, as he is one of my sets of eyes and ears. Not that Knox knows that. Epaphras enters the room with a scowl. "Yes, sire?"

Knox looks confused until I grin at him and he just shakes his head at me. "Epaphras, do you know where Valdís is currently?"

"Yes. She has just gone back to her rooms a bit ago, as you arrived actually," he gives me a hard stare and I grin back unrepentant, "she had been in the kitchen eating and visiting with Cook."

Knox nods, "Yes, that's right. Cook is one of her family employees' cousin. He is the one that passed the letters from his cousin to us. I need to thank him for that. You say she is in her room again?"

"Yes. If there is nothing else you require of me, I am quite busy right now with unplanned room readying," he says as he glares at me. Snickering, I turn my face away. I hear him turn and exit the room. As the door clicks shut, Knox bursts with laughter.

"I haven't seen him so mad in years! What did you do?"

Still grinning, I tell him, "I didn't let him know I would be home early. He is mad because my room isn't ready already."

Knox stands, shaking his head at me. "You can't be making the people that keep the castle running mad. We are all going to end up with something vile in our shoes. Come on, I'll take you to meet her."

I didn't really believe him when he said the room accepted her until he led me to our wing. Straight to the door I had begun to pray would never open. Directly to the concentration of the best scent I have ever smelled. Right toward the woman I can't accept.

He knocks on the door and I hear her say come in. The guards on either side of her door are ramrod straight, as though they can sense my mood. Knox opens the door and a wave of her scent hits me. The smell of her makes me weak. Which is exactly why I cannot have anything to do with her. I was weak once and my brothers paid for it.

I follow him, keeping my eyes on the floor until he stops and says, "Valdís, I want to introduce you to my brother, Malic."

I finally look at her, and I am lost, her olive skin and curves. That long dark hair. She stands from the chair she was sitting in and extends her hand. "Hello, it's nice to meet you. My, you smell as good as Knox does. Are you guys bathing in something?" Knox laughs as I struggle to make my hand obey me. Reaching out, I take her hand and the contact hits us both. Raw energy surging between us as she clasps my rough hand with her soft one. Her eyes drift closed and her mouth forms an oh as the scent of her arousal fills the air.

Then I snatch my hand from hers. "I will see you tomorrow. I have many questions for you about the current situation." With that, I turn and leave the room as fast as I can.

I hear her behind me asking Knox in a breathy voice, "What was that?"

As I shut the door behind me, he answers, "That was a man running from his destiny."

Two

My brother's reaction to Valdís only confirms my suspicions. She is the queen that our goddess promised us so long ago. The queen we had given up hope would appear. Now she is here, and we only found her because her people were in danger from her mother. I need to find out more about her family and why they would go to such lengths to keep her from inheriting. Even for an abuser, this seems drastic. Blowing holes in the castle walls, kidnapping her, having her declared mentally unfit.

But first, I inhale deeply as I take the two steps to stand close to her. "Valdís, I can smell how much touching him, even that little bit turned you on. Would you like me to take care of that for you before I go tend to some things that need... done?"

Her breath escapes her like she was holding it. "Isn't it weird for you? That your brother did that to me?"

I laugh as I run my fingertips lightly up her arms. "First, we aren't that kind of brother. There are no family ties between any of us. We were all from separate tribes. Second, there is only one queen's room. I think the real question here is, is this weird for you? There are more of us..." I let my words trail off as I run a hand along her shoulder and up into her hair, gripping it and tipping her head back, leaning down I murmur in her ear, "Are you bothered by the idea of more than one man? Would being worshiped by kings make you uncomfortable?"

Her heart is beating fast and her breath coming in little pants, her hands gripping my shirt. She whispers, "I think I could get right with it."

I grin as I ease her back down into the chair she had been sitting in. I push the flowing skirt she is wearing up her thighs, her eyes dark as she watches my hands bunching the fabric. The material bunched at her hips as I lift it, revealing her bare pussy. A low growl escapes my throat as I lower my face to bury it in her hot, sweet lips. Letting go of her skirt, I grab her thighs and shove them into the air as I lick the honey from her slick hole. Her little gasps are driving me wild. I drag my tongue up her pussy to her clit and her body convulses.

I look up at her, "Like that, do you?"

She groans, "Oh Goddess yes, yes I do."

I let her thighs rest on my shoulders and I take one finger to her sweet pussy, lightly edging around it before I slip it in. She moans as I withdraw it and then slide two fingers in. I keep my fingers at a slow pace, fucking her with them as her hips roll with it, trying to take me in deeper.

Watching her ride my hand is a fucking dream I never want to wake from, so I lean down and circle her clit with my tongue. She grabs my hair and holds tightly, moaning, "Oh sweet Goddess, yes! Don't stop!" I suck her clit hard then, and she screams with pleasure. Fucking her faster with my fingers till she is incoherent, riding my fingers as I follow her, keeping the suction hard on her clit. When I flick my tongue across it and her body tenses for a second before she convulses, her pussy grabbing my fingers over and over. She rips my mouth from her clit, "Too much, too much, can't. Oh fuck me, oh Goddess, that was good. Fuck me, Knox. I want your cock in me while my pussy is still looking for something to hold on to."

She doesn't have to ask me twice. I rip the front of my pants open and ease into an upright position, keeping her legs against my chest as I fist my cock with the other hand. Lining it up, I drive it all the way in till my hips hit her ass. She lets out a strangled cry and I pause. Her eyes fly open. "Fuck me, Knox! Fuck me hard now!"

Never one to deny such a fantastic request, I withdraw all but the tip and I start fucking her hard and fast. Her every cry and moan drives me to new heights. I open her legs and, holding them out, I tell her, "Touch yourself. Touch yourself while I fuck you, Valdís."

Her hand leaves the arm of the chair she has been clutching and she rubs her clit in fast circles. It is the hottest thing I have ever seen. I can't hold on much longer and then she comes with a thump, her pussy clamping down on my cock over and over. I can't hold back any longer and I bury myself in her, coming inside her as her pussy massages my cock with her orgasm.

I lean down and lay my head on the back of the chair as we both try to cope with the world after that. She laughs softly. "I might be all right with kings worshiping me, but if it involves a lot of this, I might die of pleasure. I mean, what a way to go. And I am not sad about the idea. Definitely a level or thirty above the way other people want me to die."

I laugh to cover up the fear that shoots through my body at the thought of her dying, however it happens. We have to get the rest of the kings here so they can accept her, then she will be protected in a way that we can't protect her. If everything the Goddess said was accurate. It has to be. It can't be any other way.

I ease back, my cock finally leaving her body. She starts to sit up, mumbling something about going to clean up. I push her gently back into the seat, "Wait here, I will get a cloth and tend to it." Her eyes bug out as I get up and go to her bathroom, faster than I really needed to so I can get back before she tries to come do it herself.

I make it back as she is starting to sit up again, I put a

hand on her shoulder and press her back into the seat with a grin. Then I clean her very thoroughly with the cloth, making her gasp in pleasure a few times. She smiles as I toss the cloth to the side and then moans loudly as I give her pussy one more long kiss. I pull her skirt down, telling her, "I could easily stay here all day with you, but I really need to get some things done today."

She leans forward and gives me a long kiss goodbye. The beast in me growls. I want to take her again, but protecting her is more important. So I withdraw from her fiery kisses and tell her, "We'll talk about this more later."

Leaving the room, I speak with her guards briefly, checking the schedule for who will be with her for the rest of the day, just so I know. My mind at ease that our best will be with her, I head for the records room. Hopefully, also to some answers.

Eirene

Rising in the morning is so much nicer without Conrí and his incessant need to go tend to our people. I haven't bothered with them since he died and yet they are fine. Figuring things out themselves and still paying their rents. To think, he spent all that time riding around and helping them, babying them more like!

Never letting them fend for themselves as they should have been.

Ah, there is Flaviana with my tea. I feel a presence enter my room and I know it is him. I take my coffee from her and shoo her out of the room, telling her I will call her when I need her.

As soon as she is gone and the door closed I speak, "My Lord, how can I serve you?"

"You can make your daughter queen. I have seen it. She must be queen if we are to succeed."

"I thought we were trying to get rid of the kings?"

"Yes, most of them. But the path to our success has your daughter marrying the High King, Vincent."

I sip my coffee as I ponder this. "How will I arrange this? It's not like I am friends with the kings."

"You will position your daughter as a strong leader, one that would have you always as her advisor. The people of the island will distrust the kings, and your lackeys will have them killed. But at just the right time, you will step in and save King Vincent. As a reward, you will ask that he marry your daughter."

"But if the entire island mistrusts the kings, how will that work? Won't it put my daughter in danger?"

"No. You will have her positioned as a native of this land, younger, from an excellent family, and with the ability to sway this last king into doing the things that will be best for this island country. Because obviously this island suffers with only ancient men ruling it, holding fast to their ancient, bloodthirsty ways."

"I see. I think I can make this happen. So I will start appearing publicly with my daughter, appearing in advisory capacity to her as far as the rest of the island is concerned. But the king, I am to save him?"

"Yes. When it comes time, I will give you a weapon to do so. You will further our aims by telling people what a shame it is that the kings have not lived a normal continuation of their lives, marriage, children, passing on the monarchy. You put a focus on how the island could progress and not be closed off from the rest of the world if things were done in a regular manner instead of this crazy eternal monarchy. In the meantime, plant this next to the driveway of the castle." A plant that looks like Crown of Thorns appears on my dresser.

I ask, "What will it do?"

He says, "It will keep them in the castle. All of the castles will be cut off from the rest of the island as long as that one plant is in the ground."

I toast the air with my coffee cup as I say, "Your will be done." His presence is gone just like that, not even so much as a goodbye. I suppose I can't expect human niceties from a god, but it would be nice. I hit the button to call Flaviana back in and have a start to my day.

Ingemar

. . .

The wine isn't fixing it. I just haven't found the right amount yet. Refilling my glass, I peer at the bottle when the flow stops before the cup is full. Shit, it's empty. I toss it away from me. It thumps on the carpeted floor. My glass is empty again with one swig. Reaching into the cabinet, I grasp nothing. I lean down and peer into the dim space. It is emptied of bottles and straightening, I see the litter of many bottles scattered across the floor. But I still hear that voice in my head. That voice that came out of thin air at her command.

My head rings with it still. The fear, the horror of the whole thing. More wine. I need more wine. "Hulthen!" My shout dies off when the door opens until it reveals my son Pelos. He was completely useless when the king was here. When we dispose of the kings, he will not be the new king. He is as weak as my wife. She is nearly on her deathbed at this point, what with the poison I have been slowly feeding her.

Perhaps I will take Valdís to wife when the kings are gone. I feel certain that the kingship will be offered to me. If my son happens to go in the process of taking back the kingdom well, that will make things much more tidy. Pelos clears his throat from before my desk. Impudent brat. Time was he would have waited till I was ready to notice him. I peer at him. "What are you here for?"

The little shit rolls his eyes at me. "If you had been listening father, I said that you seem distressed."

I stand, angry that he thinks to comment on my distress and the world goes sideways briefly. My hand hits the desk, and I am saved from an ignoble fall. Narrowing my eyes to see him better, I tell him, "Distressed? I am not distressed. I am handling my current problems with things by medicating until the urge to feel it goes away. As would you if you had been in Eirene's place when that voice started talking out of nowhere." I see the skeptical look on his face and I shake a finger at him. "I know what you are thinking. I was sober as Hulthen when it happened. The injury from the king didn't affect my faculties beyond leaving me with a black eye and bruised pride. The voice created thunder inside Conrí's office!"

Hulthen enters then, "Sir, here is the wine you requested. I took the liberty of bringing several bottles for you."

"Ah, Hulthen, bring them in, go ahead and place the extras in the cabinet, but refill my glass and leave a bottle here on the desk for me." Hulthen nods and pulls in a small cart, pushing it across the room and behind me. He is quick and efficient. We remain silent while he completes his tasks. He collects the empty bottles on his way out, barely even breaking his stride. Once the door closes behind him, I tell my son, "Sit. We will talk."

I ease myself down into my chair as Pelos seats himself. "Father, this voice, it did Eirene's bidding?"

I nod, "Yes. Well, now that I think about it, I think the voice was merely backing her right then. Perhaps the voice is the one in charge? Why do you ask?"

"Well, it would seem that if Eirene is the uniting factor, getting rid of her would solve the issue, yes?"

I nod and take a healthy swig from my glass. Swallowing as I ponder this more, "Getting rid of her would solve the issue. But we need her backing while we get rid of the kings. Her support, as it is one of her daughters, is important."

He puts a hand on his chin, thinking. I swear the creature turning the crank for his thoughts must be drunker than I am. I drain and refill my glass before he looks up and says, "But once the kings are gone, we won't need her, right? At that point we can dispose of her?"

Good Lady, he is slow, and I am the drunk one. "Yes, at that point, it would be very convenient for her to have an accident of some sort." More convenient if you were with her.

"Then it sounds like we only need to tolerate this voice until we get rid of the kings. How much longer before that is done?"

I rested my forehead on the heel of one hand. "Son, this is still something we are working on. It is still in the planning stages. There is no timeline for it yet."

"Oh. Can I help in some way, father? We could sketch out plans together?"

"Thank you, son, but a few more things need to happen and I must collect the information from those before we can further make plans. Have you checked on your mother today? She seems to be wasting away. I just don't understand it."

Pelos nods. "I was with her earlier. She seems to be slipping away. I don't understand what good are the doctors if they can't figure this out? She is much too young to waste away like this."

"She is too young to waste away, but sometimes it happens. Some people are just not meant to live as long as we tend to. The outsiders we used to allow in, they live barely a fraction of our lives. Perhaps she is just too delicate, too fragile to take the strain of a life that long."

He nods, "I'm sure that is it father, she is very delicate seeming. I was afraid as a child that if I hugged her too hard, she would somehow break. I will spend time with her as often as I can. Perhaps it will cheer her."

"Yes, I think that would cheer her. She adores you, her only child. You should go, spend time with her. I will be back to working on things tomorrow. Tonight is for seeing how much wine I will be able to drink. Have a good night, son."

Three

Knox left me clean and tucked in this massive bed once again. I was feeling sleepy, like I might drift off until the door closed. Now, my doubts plague me. Because honestly, what is someone whose own mother couldn't love her doing in the queen's suite thinking that a king could be that interested in her?

I have to get them to take care of my people. Whatever game they are playing with me, it doesn't matter. I'll talk to Knox today, see if he will at least send someone to check on them, see to their welfare. Maybe Malic would... no. I just want to see him again. See if he was as blown away by our hands touching as I was. The thoughts just keep circling in my mind and after a time I decide that if I will not sleep I am not going to lie in this bed alone with how my thoughts are going. But what am I going to do? Wander the castle aimlessly? No. I am not wandering about like some sad puppy with no playmates. Cook! I'll go see Cook!

My plan set I hurry to get dressed, a simple pair of black pants that are loose and flowing down the legs paired with a fitted white top. A pair of sandals and I am sailing out the door. The guards jumped when I passed them before they scrambled to catch up. I might have to surprise them more often.

Knox

My questions about where Valdís came from have led me to the place I have avoided ever since we started wandering the world in an attempt to bury our pain at not getting to love the queen we were promised. The records room is where we kept all the tales. Both the true and the untrue. We laid our tellings of what led us to being kings here. My brothers in arms that died, their words live on here. Not that I have been able to step foot down here or even think about reading any of what they wrote. We stashed their journals down here too. I realize I am still standing in front of the closed door. I haven't even touched the doorknob. Swallowing, I step forward and grasp the knob, turning it and pushing the door open. I find the light switch next to the door and flip it up, closing my eyes as the room explodes into light.

Opening them, I am greeted with a room that looks deceptively ordinary. A computer dominates a table in the middle of the room. It connects to a plug in the middle of the floor under it. That computer holds all the digitized copies of our records. At least, the ones that have made it in there. We have been lax about getting the really old records into digital format. On the far side of the room is a wall of bookshelves filled with our old journals. Lining the rest of the walls are large filing cabinets. Each marked with the years contained within. Being in here, seeing the journals, it feels like my heart bleeds with the pain of the loss of my brothers in arms again. We are not related, but they are more family to me than my own is. None of the family I was born into live still. Oh, there are descendants, of course, but they are far removed from me, and that was how they wanted it.

Realizing that I am still standing in the door ruminating instead of searching the records, I step into the room and quickly cross to the computer. Tapping the mouse so the screen lights up, I type in the password. I begin my search with Conrí Potentus. His lineage comes up, his family line goes back to the founding tribes. I remember many of his family. They were good people. Now for her mother. I check Conrí's marriage announcement, her maiden name is omitted. That is curious. Why wouldn't that be there? I see no mention of her parents either. The usual celebration of things like this includes both families. Even if the parents are dead, they are still included. Another hour passes before I finally find a mention of her last name, Scheklebergen. That is an odd last name for an Atlantean family. She couldn't be an outsider. I would have noticed the mark on Valdís. Inputting the last name into a search, I come up with exactly nothing. There should be something. Records of her parent's death. Or birth. Marriage. Her grandparents even. But the search returns nothing. I look at the file cabinets as my body fills with dread. So many files.

Sighing, I stand and head for the cabinet with the most recent hundred years in it. The lack of records for this family is unusual enough to be heavily concerning. Our people have been recording their lineage, their joyful moments, and their sorrows since the time of the great battle. I can't even imagine what would cause a family... no. I can imagine some things. But I don't like the ideas that come to mind for why they would want to keep from being noticed.

Malic

I had Epaphras meet me in my office, the one that isn't the more public king's office. I need more information about this Valdís. This woman that sends electricity surging through my body with just the touch of her hand.

Valdís that smells of all the good things, who I want to inhale so deeply she becomes part of me. Feeling a strange pain in my pants, I realize my cock has grown hard just thinking about her. I adjust it out of the painful angle it was in just before Epaphras walks back into my office with the letters he had gone to fetch.

As he was telling me all he knew about this woman, he casually mentioned that the woman that had worked for their family all this time, that had spent much of her time protecting Valdís from her own mother, had been writing letters to our Cook, her cousin, all this time. Those letters had come into our possession recently when Cook mentioned having saved them, and now I would read them. He sets a rather thick file on the desk before me, keeping his hand flat on top of it. He says, "I know you will read this in its entirety. I want to remind you that these people have already attacked the castle twice in an attempt to carry out what they started here, but in a more desperate fashion. Whatever you think of Valdís, I was there when she was told of these letters. I don't know if she knows about all of this. More to the point, I don't know if she should know about all of this."

His piece said he removes his hand and steps back to have a seat. I look at the file and back up at him. "What do you mean, you don't know if she should know about all this?"

"Sire, read the file. I think you will understand as you go." He looks away from me and presses his lips together. I know he won't say more without my forcing the issue, so

I open the file. The first letter is from nearly seventy years ago. This woman writes of her horror at walking into the child's room after seeing the mother leave it and finding a baby Valdís blue and unresponsive. She massaged the child and blew air into her lungs over and over until she started breathing again, all the while praying to our Goddess that she send this child back. She goes on to tell her cousin that the child cried in fear every time her mother came anywhere near her after that and how she worked with two other servants to ensure the mother was rarely, if ever, left alone with the child again.

Page after page, I read terrible things. Valdís' mother has been trying to kill her all her life. Most of the attempts would have seemed like accidents, taken alone or without the witness of one of the employees. I come to a page roughly a quarter of the way through the stack and I see that Conrí caught her trying to murder their daughter. She was supposed to still be resting after the birth of their second daughter, but instead was attempting to drown their eldest daughter in a fountain. While this woman and another servant held young Valdís and dried her and her tears, Conrí hit his wife once, a resounding slap to her face. The control he displays in only hitting her once is astounding. I start skimming the pages. Conrí never forgave his wife for trying to murder their daughter, and if the letters are to be believed, he became a target after Valdís was grown.

I finish the file and look at Epaphras, "She hasn't seen these?"

"No sire, I was there when Cook told her of the existence of these letters. I spoke to her guards from that day as well. She didn't know they were related or that the cousin had been writing to Cook all this time. She had found out just a little before I arrived. As I said earlier, when she came to the castle, she was on the run and begging for the Kings to help her people. Not her, she fully expected to die for the asking. But was still willing to come here and die so long as the people her father had been tending all these years were kept safe from her mother's neglect and possible malice."

"There is no way anyone is that good and so many people want her dead. It doesn't make any sense. Nobody that selfless has that many people with a vendetta against them. She has to be hiding something."

Epaphras' face is carefully noncommittal as he says, "I suppose that is possible, sire, but it seems less than likely in this case. She has her faults, but none that appear vile enough to have her killed for. Perhaps they know something we do not know about her? If so, what? She has been guarded the entire time she has been here. None of her behavior has been suspicious, and she doesn't display the traits of a bully or sociopath."

"Hmm, yes. I need to talk to Cook. I need to hear about his cousin and how trustworthy she is, or if she could be delusional."

Epaphras' brows draw down, making him look rather raptor like, "Sire, you seem. How do I put this? Determined perhaps? Bullheaded? Blind about the possibility that everyone else here is reading the situation exactly right. Respectfully, this woman and her people need protection. Whatever may be going on for you regarding this woman that is clouding your judgment, it isn't befitting that a king be so blindly focused on only one possibility."

Scrubbing a hand across my face, I try to get myself together. I want to be mad about what he said, to shout the lie of it to the heavens. And I can't. I am focused on proving this woman to be something other than the beacon she is for me. I am desperate to find some reason why she is not right, why I must stay away from her and all I keep finding are reasons why she needs our protection even more than I need to pretend she isn't the one. Our queen.

Looking back to Epaphras I say, "I will give her a chance Epaphras. I just want to be thorough first."

"Yes, sire. Do you require anything else?"

"No, I know where to find Cook. Thank you. For the assistance and the check on my attitude."

He dips his head slightly at me, "Happy to be of service, sire." Then he opens the door to my office and is gone.

Staring at the open door for a moment, I try to collect myself. To brace against the scent of her that I know I will encounter as I move through the castle. One last deep breath and I hoist myself up to seek out Cook.

Four

MALIC

I was right in thinking that her scent would be throughout the halls. It only grows stronger as I draw near the kitchen. The closer I get, the stronger my suspicion is that she is in the kitchen now. I stop outside the door, half decided to put it off till later when I hear Cook say, "I've been reading the letters my cousin wrote me all these years and it has left me with one question. How did your father allow it all to happen? How is it that only those few employees helped you? Why didn't he protect you from her?"

I hear her shift in her seat and Cook moving around as he waits for her to answer. She finally says, "It only happened when he was gone. I told you that he was often out helping our people, and that meant he wasn't home a lot of the time. So that left me with my mother and those employed by my father, and eventually my sister was part of my mother's cadre as well. I know she has always hated me." I can hear what sounds like her picking at the finish on the table as she speaks. In my mind, I imagine her focusing intently on picking at the table so she doesn't see the pity in Cook's expression.

"If what I have been told is true, she has been trying to kill me almost as long as I have been alive. It stands to reason that she probably did, considering how many times I remember her trying to kill me. I remember one time when she took my sister and I out for a picnic. She made me go with her to look at this old hole left by hunters a long time ago. Next thing I know, I am waking up in the bottom of the hole and there is no one around to hear me scream. They found me the next day, though. My father was so happy to find me. He just held me close for hours."

Cook drops a knife. The clatter is excruciating, and exclaims, "That really happened? I thought Dagma was just making shit up at that point. What mother goes out with two children, comes back with one, and doesn't damn mention that one is gone?"

She chuckles ruefully, "Mine apparently. Dad instituted a child check at some point after that. When that didn't work out so great, he made a rule that my mother was not allowed to leave the house with me alone and that my sister did not count as not being alone. He specified that it had to be another full-grown adult. She raged over the indignity of it for days."

Cook swears rather creatively for a bit as he slams dishes about. I'm kind of impressed. Then he says, "Dagma wrote to me once and told me this story about finding you half dead washed up on the shore. If you would, tell me how they came to find you there? How old were you then?"

"Oh. That one. Um. Yes, I can tell you." The pain in her voice. I have to restrain myself from going to comfort her. "We were at a seaside vacation place, it was holidays. So we had a fancy dinner that night, lots of people there. It was grand. We were all dressed up, and I was thirteen. I felt so beautiful and grown in the dress my dad and Dagma had made for me. Then we sat down at the dinner and after I started eating, I didn't feel so well. It came on suddenly. So I excused myself and Dagma tucked me into bed. I fell asleep quickly and when I woke I was not in my bed. One of the people my mother had hired was carrying me, walking behind her. They had me thrown over their shoulder. I don't know who it was, really. I never saw their face I just assume that it was one of hers because they were going along with it."

Cook says, "A reasonable assumption."

"The vacation house was near this enormous cliff," I hear Cook gasp and a ball of dread forms in my stomach. I read this in the letters, but they didn't mention the cliff. She goes on, "I thought maybe if I pretended to still be knocked out, I would have a chance to run away. But they stopped, and he flipped me over his shoulder into his arms. I heard her tell him, toss her in. Then I fell forever. My screams echoed back at me as I fell. The water was ice. I don't remember a whole lot after I hit the water. I was sinking and then I saw lights and I thought it was all over, so I just let go. When I woke again, I was on the beach and surrounded by people. I thought I would never be warm again. But eventually I was warm. I never slept in my bed when I was ill again, though."

I hear Cook's movement stop as he says, "Where do you sleep when you are ill?"

She responds, "Different places. Since my dad died, I don't really sleep in any one place ever."

Five

VALDÍS

He has been outside the kitchen eavesdropping for a long time now. I guess he really wanted to know the sordid details of some of the times my mother tried to murder me. Weird, but maybe he has reasons. I wonder how much longer—

The door behind me hits the wall and we all jump. I turn to see him striding in, jaw clenched and looking like he wants to murder someone. He points at Cook. "I'll be questioning you later. Expect the summons." He turns that pointing finger at me and I swallow as he says, "You. You, I have many more questions than I do answers about you, and you can come now to be questioned. Since you are out wandering the castle, you can be useful."

I don't know what possessed me at this point, but

something about his tone struck a chord in me and I suddenly felt contrary. Why is he being so nasty to me when I haven't been even a little bit uncooperative? Since I met him, he has been rude and fuck that. I stand slowly and walk over to Cook in careful measured steps while everyone watches. He has the nerve to growl at me as I reach to hug Cook, stopping me in my tracks. Turning to face him, I say, "I don't care who you are. If you can't be polite to me, this is going to take all day. I am suddenly starting to feel hungry. I might need to wait for some food."

He stomps over to lean down into my face and tell me, "If you don't get moving, I am going to throw you over my shoulder and carry you out of here. Don't try me Princess!"

I snarl right back at him, "You touch me without permission and it will be a pleasant summer's day in the frozen reaches of the Underworld before I tell you anything! If you want me to answer your damn questions, you are going to have to ask me nicely! You don't need to know about me to know my people need help. Help which you could be providing if you weren't on this kick to know about me."

I watch his eyes as he assesses the room and glares back at me. "Fine, Princess," he grits out from teeth clenched so hard I fear they'll break, "Will you please get your ass to my office so that I can question you?"

Folding my arms across my chest, I stare at him, watching the little vein in his forehead throb. "Your manners are still poor, but it's a start." I hug Cook and tell him I will see him soon before I walk out of the kitchen, my guards following. They are stopped by him in the kitchen and I just wait in the hall as he tells them they aren't needed for this.

I think it is the barrel chested one that tells him, "Forgive us, Sire, but King Knox ordered us to stick with her, even if he was her escort."

I hear him growl fine and then he pushes through the door with my guards and stops to stare at me like I did something wrong by not being in his office already. Shrugging, I tell him, "I don't know where your office is."

It is all I can do to keep my poker face in place as he narrows his eyes at me before starting down the hall with a terse "Follow me" thrown over his shoulder.

I grin at my guards and rush to catch up. Drawing even with him, I ask my burning question, "So how long were you standing outside the kitchen listening, anyway?"

Malic

I manage not to stumble when she asks how long I was listening outside the kitchen, but it is a close thing. So I ignore the question and we get to my office. I hold the door open for her to enter and I tell her guards, "You can wait out here," just before I enter the room and shut the door in their faces. When I turn, she is seating herself before the desk and I hurry to get behind it. Her face reads calm but her scent says nervous and turned on. Breathing her in was a mistake. I need to be near to her. I want to comfort her and fuck her senseless. What is wrong with me? I know I can't do this. I must be strong.

Walking back around the desk, I sit one hip on the corner of the desk and glare at her, unreasonably annoyed that I feel such a need to be close to this infuriating woman.

Then she smiles up at me, "Did you enjoy listening at the door like some run-of-the-mill eavesdropper? Did you find out things you didn't know or just more about a story that gave you questions?"

How does she know? She couldn't have known I was out there. No one else knew. I saw the surprise on Cook's face and on her guards. But now that I think about it, she jumped for the noise but looked back slowly... "How did you know I was out there?"

Her lips twist wryly, "Because I can smell you coming down the hall. Because your scent calls to me, the same as Knox's scent does."

"Wait, you knew I was out there the entire time?"

She nods her head once. "I did. I kept waiting for you to come in, but you just seemed to want to hang outside the door like a creeper and who am I to say you can't do that in your own castle?"

I don't know how to respond to that. I certainly can't

tell her that listening to what her mother did to her made me so angry I thought about going to her home to put an end to most of our issues right then. And I can't tell her it took a lot of my energy to keep my hands unclenched in order to stop from injuring myself. I can't tell her I would stand anywhere just to get to breathe her in or that her scent keeps me hard constantly. Even now, I have to keep my cock tucked off to one side in the hope that no one notices. "When the guard was carrying you to the cliff, did you realize where they were taking you?"

"No. It was just grasses beneath me. I never thought," she turns her face away from me and takes a breath, "it never occurred to me that she would have me thrown off a cliff into the ocean. I guess it should have. But it didn't."

"Where was she when they found you?"

"She was standing above me looking down, and I knew if I said anything about how it happened, she would make me pay. My father was asking me right then what I was doing in the water at night. I knew from the way her face twisted that if I said anything, she would make it so much worse for me than I could ever imagine."

"I see. Did the attacks slow as you got older?"

"Some. But that may be because it was too difficult to figure out where I would be each night. Or because I became adept at hiding within our house and even better at reading the atmosphere there." She squirms in her chair like she can't quite get comfortable. How did she hide so well if she can't even sit in a chair for a time without squirming?

"I know your father died recently. You have my condolences. He was a good person. Tell me about how he died, if you can speak of it?"

She squirms in her chair again. "Yes, I can speak of it. He was home with us and a stranger came to the house and said that one of our more remote people needed help desperately. The pump for the well had been destroyed by something, and it was their only source of water. When the messenger was telling us this, my father suddenly looked at my mother and I followed his gaze. She had a small smile on her face till she realized my father was looking at her. Then it was blank, cold. He gave me directions I didn't understand when he left. They made sense when word came that he had died. The rest, well, you know as much or maybe more than I do. They supposedly filed the report with the office in town, and I was told that a copy is always sent to the castle as well. The will hadn't been read at that point and no one knew I was heir, so they gave my mother the copies of those documents and I did not get to see them."

She is squirming in her chair again. How did she hide so well if she must move so much? Goddess, her scent is driving me crazy. "When—"

"I need to take a break," she says as she near jumps up from the chair.

"No! I am not done questioning you. You will stay right here, sit down!"

This woman gets right in my face and says, "Unless you are going to take care of the raging inferno in my pants, you can damn well wait till I get back!" Then she really turns and walks toward the door.

This fire flares to life in me. Why does she have an inferno? Who is it she wants? I am off the desk and snatching her up against me in an instant. "Who is causing this inferno?"

She narrows her eyes at me and yells, "You are! Your scent is driving me insane with need, you fucking asshole! How has this not seeped into your thick skull yet? You are causing the inferno and I need some space before I combust or tear your damn clothes off and have my way with you!"

Hunger rears its head and I don't know whether I want to bite her or fuck her or both. I do know that I am not safe for her right now, no matter how much I want to see if she would try to rip my clothes off. I set her away from me. "Go. Take the damn guards and go. I'll talk to you more later." When she doesn't immediately start to move, I shout at her, "Go!"

Ingemar

I stare at the note in my hand as I wait for Pelos to get to my office. I sent Hulthen after him just moments ago. And I have no idea where he is. Possibly with his mother. She is nearly dead.

The note is what concerns me right now, though. Eirene has sent for both of us to attend to her at her home. The last time I was there still rings through my mind sometimes. I know we must go and for the time being; she is effectively running the show.

I will be watching for our opportunity to get rid of her and her strange voice from nowhere. I feel certain that her strange voice or power from wherever will be gone with her, as she seems to be the only connection. Pelos enters without knocking, his expression sour. "Father, why must we both attend to this woman? Surely she would be content with just you, considering I am sitting with my mother as she dies."

"You know why! We must seem bent to her will until an opportunity presents itself. The only way to do that is to go along with her plans for now, as they mostly coincide with our own, anyway. Now, tell your mother you will return as soon as possible and get to the car."

Pelos pouts and kicks at the carpet before finally saying, "Yes, Father, I will meet you there."

I watch him leave. My door left standing open as he strides off down the hall toward his mother. He is entirely too bold, too arrogant lately. Something will need to be done about it.

VALDÍS

I just wanted out of there for a little bit so I could collect myself. But this, Goddess, he must be disgusted by the fact that I want him. I open the door and slip out, racing to get as far away from there as possible. The tears are burning and filling my eyes before I get to the end of the hall. Why couldn't he just let me go? Why did he have to make me admit I want him so badly and then reject me? Is it some sick game he likes to play?

My face is wet and I feel the tears running down my neck, soaking my collar. I wish I was still in the room far away from the kings. I wouldn't have to try to cope with the scent of someone that turns me on so much and wants me not at all.

Knox steps out of his office and sees me. He reaches

out and I duck out of reach as I walk past him. "I don't want to talk about it, Knox. Just leave me alone."

Taking off running, though it wouldn't do any good if he wanted to catch me. I still run the rest of the way to my room and shut myself inside. I head straight for the bathroom and that massive tub.

Knox

I smell Malic on Valdís as she rushes past me in tears, saying she doesn't want to talk about it, her guards hot on her heels. What the hell did he do? It hasn't even been that long! I recall he planned to question Valdís today and I start toward his office. Just as I get to his door, he is exiting the room, looking like a storm about to break. I stop and lean against the wall. "Malic, what did you do?"

He manages to deepen his scowl as he says, "What are you talking about?"

I pretend to focus on my nails as I ask, "What did you do to her? What did you do that had her running to her room in tears? Is that how you protect us now? By hurting our — by hurting women?"

I watch as his expression changes, his eyes widening and his jaw dropping. He didn't notice my slip, thankfully. He closes and opens his mouth a few times before saying, "What do you mean? She wasn't crying when she left."

I watch his eyes as I tell him, "I just passed her in the hall. She was crying and wouldn't even stop for me. But I could smell you on her." I push off the wall and stand in front of him, my arms crossed in front of my chest, "So again I ask, what did you do?"

Malic runs a hand across the back of his neck and sighs. "I was questioning her. She was sitting in a chair here in my office. Then she was jumping up, talking about needing a break, and I told her no. She insisted she had to go, said something about my scent doing things..."

His sentence trails off and I suddenly have an idea of what might have happened. "She told you that your scent was turning her on, driving her crazy. And locked up in that little office. No fucking wonder. I can only imagine what her scent was doing to you. Locked up in your little office alone with her, she would be screaming my name to the heavens. You obviously didn't go that route, or if you did, we need to talk about your technique." he glares at me hard for that. "So that leaves your mouth. What did you say to her?"

"I told her to go and take her guards with her."

"Yeah. What else? I told you I could smell you on her. Tell me so I can go convince her that you aren't as much of an asshole as you seem to be."

He sighs and looks at the wall like it might jump at him. "I might have snatched her up against me when she tried to leave. And it was while I had her pressed against me that she told me how much my scent was affecting her and that I needed to fix it or let her go. I was a little concerned at that point about my reaction and I set her away from me before I told her to go and take her guards with her."

I shake my head. "Let me make sure I am seeing this scene correctly. This gorgeous woman who smells like everything good in our lives tells you that your scent is doing things to her and she tries to leave. You envelope her in your scent, press her against your body, and make her explain exactly what she means by that. Then, then you set her away from you like she disgusts you and you tell her to go away?" He nods, looking as miserable as I have seen him in a long time. "So you really made her condition worse. I know you could smell how turned—or could you? Can you distinguish her being turned on from her regular scent?" He shakes his head no while still looking hard at the wall. "Ok. Well, you need practice. Personally, I think the best practice is burying your face between those thighs but to each their own. I am going to go fix this. We are all, yes you too, all going to have dinner together in a few hours. You get your shit together and find a way to be nice to her tonight. Whether or not you are ready to admit it, that is our future queen. The three of us aren't the only ones you will crush if you chase her away."

I turn away and head for her room. I hear him take off the other way down the hall, trying and failing at not stomping away like an angry child. However, I'm not worried about him. It's Valdís I worry about right now.

Valdís

The tub is filled with steaming hot water, but still my tears feel hot on my face as I sit here. Maybe I shouldn't take it so personally that he doesn't want me when he has such an effect on me. But all I can seem to think about is how many people don't want me. My mother most of all. If what I see around me is to be believed, that is that one person in all your life that should love you no matter what. Failed a test? Mom loves you. Fell out of a tree? Mom is there for you. Heart broken, Mom. But not me. My mother has been trying to murder me since I was born. And my sister hates me. My father's best friend sees me as a tool for breeding and property acquisition.

Maybe I should just let them have what they want? Well, my mother anyway. I'm not breeding the next generation for anyone.

All I would have to do is leave the castle and go home. One night of sleeping in my own bed and she will have me dead and buried. Everyone would be happier. I mean, obviously I am just screwing up the king's entire lives. Usually it is only one in residence at a time, but now Malic is here and Knox isn't going anywhere. I'm holding him back from living his life.

The door opens and I jump, splashing water on my face. When I open my eyes again, Knox is climbing into the tub with me fully clothed! "Knox, what are you doing? You're going to ruin your shoes and clothes!"

He just raises a brow at me. "How? With what? It's just water and everything will dry, eventually. Besides," he pulls me into his arms and lays my head on his chest, causing fresh, hot tears to flow, "you are so much more important than a few items."

Hearing that just causes me to sob and he holds me close while I cry. Eventually, my tears slow and fade into nothing. He is still holding me close and though the water is cooling, I would stay here forever. Then he moves me to the side and just when I think he will get out and leave me here, he pops the drain and turns on the hot water. He leans back and tucks me in close again. I struggle not to cry until I feel him kick off a shoe to shove the plug back in with his foot. His sock gets in the way and he curses as he pushes off the other shoe and then both his socks to operate the plug with his toes. It is such a regular human kind of dilemma that I giggle. It just bubbles up out of me. He lifts me up so he can see my face and asks, "Are you laughing at me?"

I twist around to straddle him, and I nod. "I am. It just seems so beneath a king to struggle with the drain plug. Like it should act right and plug itself when the king nudged it with his foot. It was so regular person antics and it struck me as funny that you were dealing with it."

His eyes aren't exactly focused on mine now that I am sitting on his hips and my breasts are definitely out in the open. Probably if he wasn't wearing pants, we would be having sex already at this point. He blinks and clears his throat. "Um, yes. That. Could you sit next to me? I find I can't focus on words with your tits staring at me like that. And the heat of your pussy through my pants is not helping, either."

I laugh and ease off of him. He pulls me close and tucks my head up against his shoulder again. I can't find a reason to complain. He says, "Now that my mind is clearing, I guess I understand why that struck you as funny. You can giggle again now if you like." He reaches up with his toes and turns off the water. "I talked to Malic."

I tuck my face in closer to him as I say, "Oh, you did? When does he want me to leave?"

"What? No. No leaving. He doesn't want you to leave. He is sometimes an asshole when he doesn't process his shit. We all are. I would like to say it was a product of long years with only each other for company, but I think maybe it had more to do with long years as kings. Who is going to hold us accountable for our shit? No one. Malic, he is just more of an ass than me. Maybe more than most of us. I don't know. He doesn't want you to leave, though. That I know."

"Are you sure? He looked really disgusted with me."

"I am sure. He was disgusted with himself for a lot of things right then. They did have to do with you, but not the way you think. He is all about keeping himself under control, no distractions. You, darling woman, are a hell of a distraction. If you want to know more, you will have to pry it from him. I will say, your scent has the same effect on us that our scent has on you."

"What eff—Oh. OH. I see."

"Yes, I think maybe you do now. Knowing these things, will you come to dinner tonight? It will be the three of us and Malic will behave or you can watch me throw food at him. What do you say? You could laugh at a king twice in one day."

"How could I pass up an offer like that?"

"Good. I would have felt bad dragging you in there. For now, let's just enjoy the hot water."

Seven

Eirene

I hear them in the hall talking as Flavi escorts them in here. It's tiresome how loud they are. When they are shown in, I am resting my hips on the giant desk my husband had put in here so many years ago. I keep it only because of the power it represents. If I used a prettier, more delicate desk, these fools would make me continually prove I was in charge. Thus far, I have only needed my God to back me up with Ingemar once. I intend it to stay that way.

I wait for them to seat themselves before me. Once they are looking up at me as they should, I tell them, "It is time to move forward with the campaign. Your first task is to bring a lawsuit against the kings."

I watch him squirm before he says, "What is that going to accomplish? There is no way that I will be able to win a lawsuit against the kings. That is a ridiculous idea."

My eyes roll of their own accord. "Indeed. Your case will very likely be thrown out of the court without ever being tried. But it will be on record. And the papers will find it. They will come asking about this suit. It will destroy them in popular opinion, as the papers tell everyone about the kings taking a young virginal bride away from her wedding the night before it could happen. You and your son will interview with them. You will tell them how much he adores her, how his life is broken without her. Embellish how the king forced entry into your house and assaulted you before kidnapping her." Pushing off the desk, I walk around it to stand across it from them. "When they ask about me, you will tell them I am home grieving the death of my husband and the disappearance of my daughter while trying to run the estate left behind with the daughter I have left. Lean heavily on the harm that has been created by the king's actions. Your focus throughout this should be getting Valdís back. Nothing else, is that clear?"

I watch them look at each other. Clearly, they are going to require lessons in just how bad I can make things for them, but I believe they will do this task. "After the momentum builds, you may hold rallies and post flyers. Continue to focus on getting Valdís back. Not one word about deposing the kings. Do you understand? Nothing said about deposing them."

Ingemar nods, "Yes, I understand. It will be done as you ask. Is there anything else?"

My eyes narrow as I lean forward. "Make sure you do not fuck this up. Now go. Start the process."

I watch them leave, cocky bastards. It's so hard to find good help these days.

Dagma

The warning my old friend gave me got us out of our room just in time. I hear the men clomping up the stairs as we cut through the kitchen. My friend is waiting next to the door with a bag. I usher my mother and Aunt Kalina out before me as I pause to hug her. She presses the bag into my hands. "Take this. You've been on the run too long, you are starting to lose weight you can ill afford to lose. Especially right now."

I nod and take the bag without a fight. She is right. I have been spending all I have to keep my mother and Aunt Kalina well enough that they can continue to run. I don't know how much longer we can keep this up. Thankfully, my friend has sent us to this cabin she owns, just a mile or so into the woods from her business. She is the only one that goes there and even that is infrequent. I catch up with the two old women and they are discussing where we should go next. My mother says, "What I don't understand is how they find us so fast. I know we are old, but it isn't like we are leaving a trail for them."

Aunt Kalina nods. "It is suspicious. If we had them here, I would suggest witchcraft of some sort. But that has never been something our people were capable of doing."

They both look at me as though I might have answers. I can see the exhaustion in their eyes. We can't go on like this. I sigh. "Maybe we should just go to the castle. Valdís is there and, for the first time in the past century or so, there are two kings in residence. Perhaps the kings will believe us and give us shelter, at least until Valdís comes into her inheritance. Then we can all go back to our lives."

I see the cabin through the trees as my mother says, "How do you know there are two kings in place right now? I think that might be for the best. I wasn't young when I had you. For that matter, Kalina wasn't young when she had little Philo. We aren't cut out for running all over the country anymore. It's just too much."

I avoid the question of how I know there are two kings in place right now, saying we should get going. Because I don't know how I know that, but I know it is true as sure as I know the two women before need to sleep more than anything.

We get to the cabin and after unlocking the door; I get

them settled in to catch up on some sleep. Once they are good and asleep, I make myself a cup of tea to go with a chunk of bread I ripped off what my friend put in the bag. Settling into the table, I sit down to write one more letter, just in case they show up before my friend does tomorrow.

Eight

Valdís

If I hadn't told Knox that I would go to this dinner, I would not. Well, that and knowing that he would drag me in there. I put on something that would be dressed enough for dinner with the kings but still comfortable for me considering how nervous I am. Wearing uncomfortable clothing just feels like an insult to injury with how much I don't want to go. I let Epaphras go wild with my face. He gets to do whatever as long as it will wash off later.

I think Knox maybe did not trust I would go to the dinner if left to my own devices; he isn't wrong, and he is sitting on the counter watching Epaphras work on my face. One more dusting of my face and he steps away, "Finished. And I think you will like it."

Looking at myself in the mirror, I am stunned. I know he put makeup on my face and I look amazing, but he did it so well that it is difficult for me to tell what is makeup and what isn't. I am still staring at my face when Knox hops off the counter and coming to stand next to me he says, "Come on, let's go have some food beautiful."

I nod and turn away from the mirror. I hug Epaphras even as I hear a low growl behind me, telling him, "Thank you. I feel quite lovely and I appreciate your work."

He is pale and just nods as I step back to walk away. My head tilts to one side as I study him. Realization dawns and I look at Knox. "Are you fucking kidding me? Act right! I hugged him in gratitude. King or not, you don't get to be an asshole to people over me. Or you'll wake up to hot wax on your balls, sir. As I rip it off with the least amount of care possible. Don't try me on this, Knox."

The bastard laughs at me as he takes my arm and steers me out of the room. Epaphras follows us but turns the other way down the hall. Strange, I thought it was just more of the king's rooms down there. "Knox, where does this hallway lead? If we went the other way, that is?"

"To the other king's bedrooms. The king's wings are the second most fortified places in the palaces."

Looking up at him, I ask, "The second most?"

"Yes. Second. We are here to protect the people. Being kings was just something she did as a way to give us the power to keep the ones from across the water out. She said eventually they would be able to see the continent again and we would need to trade with them. So having a governing body that they would recognize would be really important. We have been looking at how to change that. Studying other governments."

"Wait, what? I thought you all went to sleep when you weren't here? I thought in place was just a weird terminology."

We are nearing the dining area we usually go in and he sweeps me past that as he says, "Let's talk about that later. For now, here we are." He opens a door and there is a large round table, thirteen chairs circling it. Each of the chairs is well cushioned and ornate, with a small crown carved into the middle of the area behind the head.

One of the chairs has gold on the crown. That one must be for the high king? Then Knox is leading me around the table and he pulls out that chair. That chair. "Knox, what are you doing? That chair is obviously for someone important. It is the only chair with a gold inlay. I shouldn't be sitting here."

He raises a brow at me and says, "Valdís, this is your chair. You can sit in it or be sat in it. You will be sitting here to have dinner tonight, whether you think you deserve to sit here or not. How would you like to be seated?" I really contemplate throwing a fit, but he takes his hands off the chair he pulled out for me and I yelp as I jump to sit in the chair before he can do it for me. "Good girl. I'll spank you later."

"How do you know I want to be spanked?"

He smirks as he seats himself in the chair next to me. "Do you not wish to be spanked?"

I shake my head. "I didn't say I don't want it. I asked how you knew I did."

He chuckles, "Call it an educated guess, then. You certainly seem to like it if I bite you, seems a fair bet that with as sassy as you are right now, a good spanking would do things for you."

My cheeks heat with a blush, and I swallow. "Um, well, you aren't wrong."

Malic walks in then and the heat in my cheeks intensifies. He sniffs the air and narrows his eyes at Knox, then walks over to seat himself on the other side of me. Oh Goddess, I might die tonight, but what a way to go. Knox asks Malic, "Have you heard from our brethren? Do you know when they will be arriving?"

Malic looks over at him. "Why would I know that? I'm not the babysitter."

Shaking his head, Knox says, "Malic, you have been spying on all our whereabouts for as long as we have been kings. Now try again to answer the question. Any idea when our brothers will be home?" Malic growls and sends a shiver through my body along with a flood to my panties. Knox inhales and grins, "Do it again Malic, she likes it when you growl."

Malic looks surprised and his eyes flit to my face,

which is so hot I feel certain I will spontaneously combust any moment now. He inhales and manages to look more surprised. I can't take it anymore and I blurt out, "Oh, for fuck's sake, ignore me and just answer the bloody question already!"

Malic's brows draw in a bit and one side of his lips pulls up in a wry smile. "They are working on it. They don't have specific time tables yet." Then he leans toward me just a little and growls long and low. Chills run across my skin and my panties are so wet. I am just grateful my skirt is loose and black.

Malic

That scent. Fucking hell, I want to dive under the table and lick it from her center till she screams my name. Her face is bright red and the realization that she is embarrassed finally makes it through the haze of lust her scent causes in me. I want to, no; I need to fix it. How? Perhaps I could change the subject to something that doesn't do what my growl... think about that later. "Tell me, how did you come to decide to ask for help here?"

Knox eyes me. "Didn't Epaphras tell you?"

"He did, but he wouldn't necessarily remember every little detail or see as important the things I do."

The flush is fading from her face, and she smiles at

me with what looks like gratitude. I nod at her and her nervous smile of gratitude grows into a softer smile, something like she would bestow on someone she cares about. I would burn the world to ash if it would make her smile at me like that again. She is telling me about her journey from her home to the castle and all I can think is that I am terrified that I am thinking of stuff like this already. I would burn the world for a smile? What is wrong with me? I hear her telling us how Ingemar treated her, and I barely stop a growl from my throat. I want to tear him into little bits and dance with her in the remains. Why? Goddess, why would you send her now? Now? Now that we are finally coming to terms with our loneliness? That's a sick game you are playing. I realize Knox is watching me watch her. I glare at him and the bastard smiles. The first course arrives and saves me from dealing with his nonsense.

Knox finishes his first bite and asks Valdís about her mother. She tells him much the same kinds of things as she told me today when I questioned her. Then she talks about one of the employees, a Dagma. She goes on to say that this Dagma was more like a mother to her than her own ever was and that she begins to worry for her.

I ask her, "Why are you worried about her?"

She says, "Because my mother has no problems with hurting Dagma to get at me."

Well, that behavior isn't unheard of, even if it is awful. People tend toward awful. They despise the idea of us because we need blood to survive, but kill the maid to get back at your daughter, that's fine. Get the fuck out of here with that shit. "Were you close to any other employees?"

"Yes, Lommán and Quorin. My mother hated Quorin more than the other two. She threatened her any time she saw her. My mother really has never been a good person."

Knox asks before I can, "Why was she after her in particular?"

Valdís says, "Because Quorin was born Quentin and my mother said that she was an abomination. My father told her that if anything happened to her, he would have mother brought up on charges. That kept her sort of safe, but after he died, it just got worse. I kept her hidden with me a lot. She left the same night I did, before I left, so that she could go into hiding until she knew I was back. I don't think my mother would go after her, because she preferred to pretend she didn't exist and if she didn't see her, she would literally forget she existed, or at least act like she did. Lommán, she might go after him because he was like a brother to me and Dagma's son. But I think he might be better at hiding."

"I will look into where they are now. If I can find them, I will have them brought here. They should be able to corroborate your stories, and that will help when we enforce the inheritance."

Epaphras enters the dining room just then, "I'm sorry to interrupt, but you are needed, King Malic."

I look to Valdís, "Forgive me, I must go. It was a pleasure dining with you. I will keep you informed of what I find out about your loved ones."

She nods and smiles up at me, "Thank you, I really appreciate that. Could you possibly check into how my people are? I fear that without my father, they will do worse and worse until they have nothing left."

I refrain from going to my knees before her and promising to do anything she wishes. Instead, I manage a nod and tell her, "I will do that. For you."

I nearly run out of the room for fear I will embarrass myself. It is a relief that I am out of the room where all the danger lies, but I still wish I could stay in there and drink in her scent.

* * *

Epaphras and I make it far enough down the hall that Knox would not be able to hear our conversation and he starts talking, "Sire, the Cook's cousin Dagma is here. She and two older women arrived just a little while ago. She is petitioning for shelter as she says that Eirene's people have been hunting them near non stop. They have barely managed to stay a night anywhere that her people weren't forcing their way into the place and claiming they were acting as law, seeking criminals."

Grinning, I say, "Excellent. Petition granted. Take me to her, I will tell her myself. Also, I want you to see if you can find these people, they were employed at Valdís's estate. One is Lommán, Dagma's son. The other is

Quorin, she is a trans woman and Eirene has much to answer for in her treatment of this woman, Quorin. If you find them dead, have their bodies brought here. We will make sure the identity and they will have proper funerals. Have some people check into those that are dependent on Valdís's estate as well. Send crafts people that can offer aid in repairs if need be. And soldiers, in case they are attacked."

Epaphras stops at a crossing of halls and tells me, "Dagma and the mothers are in the next room to the right sire," and he heads off to the left down the hall crossing the one we got here in. A few more steps and I am entering the room where the women wait. I notice there are refreshments, but no one has touched them. The two older women look exhausted and the one I believe is Dagma is looking quite run down too.

I lean back out into the hall and whistle. A guard pops his head around the corner, sees me, and comes running. When he gets to me, I tell him, "Go get someone to prepare rooms for these women and I want the two older women escorted to their rooms as soon as they are ready. They are being granted protection for as long as they need it." The guard dips his head in acknowledgement and takes off down the hall. I turn and, walking over to the table, I pour tea for each of the women, placing baked treats on each saucer as I pass them to the women. Dagma seems reluctant to take it and I simply hold it there in front of her, waiting patiently.

One of the women, perhaps her mother, says, "Oh,

just take it already. They are not going to poison us and throw us out. And honestly, if they want to poison me with baked goods that taste a bit like heaven, I am fine with that." Dagma frowns and takes the dish from my hand.

I seat myself now that they are taken care of and I wait for Dagma to at least take a sip while the older women show no such reticence. They have warmed up considerably and are starting to whisper things to each other. They are cute and probably trouble. Dagma finally sips her tea and lets a small sigh escape her lips. Poor thing, she is probably a lot more tired than I can see. One of our servants comes to the door, knocking gently before opening and looking for me. They see me and I raise a brow in question. They nod back and I turn to the women, "Ladies, we have granted you protection. I do have more questions, but for tonight I can easily speak with just Dagma." I look at the older women, "Your rooms are ready and my friend here will take you to them. Dagma will stay and talk to me, but she will be shown where your rooms are after she leaves here. If you two would follow my friend Hilarius, they will show you to your rooms now."

The ladies set their cups on the table before them and meet my eyes for the first time, one saying, "Thank you, sire. Your hospitality is much appreciated. As is the protection."

The other one says, "Sire, would it be possible for me to see my son tonight as well?"

I smile, "Ah, so you are Kalina! Pamphilos' mother. It is a great honor to meet you and yes," I turn to Hilarius, "once you have deposited these ladies in their rooms, please see to it that Pamphilos is brought to Kalina. I know he would very much want to see his mother as soon as possible."

Hilarius nods and the ladies get up and make their way out of the room. The door closes behind them and I look at Dagma. She looks like a deer frozen in fear, eyes wide and not so much as a twitch of her fingers to indicate she is a living person. "Dagma, you have nothing to fear here, on that I give my word. Valdís was just expressing her concern for your welfare again at dinner." She still isn't moving much, but her eyes aren't so wide and she is definitely listening. "Now, would you tell me what happened after Valdís left the house that night?"

Dagma shudders and sets her cup on the table. "Yes. It, well, it wasn't good. I walked the floors waiting for her to come back with help, terrified that she wouldn't. I had heard rumors about how Lord Ingemar is and I didn't trust him. But she was determined that since that was her father's best friend, he would help her. She wouldn't hear that he might not be as true as her father had found him to be. When the knock sounded on the door, I felt a small stirring of hope until I saw it was a servant. He demanded to speak to Lady Eirene. I bade him wait while I went and woke her." She brings a hand to the side of her face. If I had to guess, I would say Eirene hit her for waking her. "When she came down to see him, he told her that Valdís had come to see Lord Ingemar with delusional tales of her mother trying to wrest an inheritance from her. They planned to marry Valdís off to Lord Ingemar's son, Pelos. They were to meet later that week to iron out the details. Once the messenger left and she had sent some of her men out to search for Valdís, she punished me. Quorin and Lommán heard my cries and left, as that was our signal. Once Lady Eirene went back to bed, I went to where I had my bag stowed and I left, heading directly for my mother's home."

She lifts her cup and drinks. I want to kill Eirene slowly. "After you reached your mother's home, did you stay there for a time?"

She holds her cup in her hands as though they are suddenly chilled. "No, sire. Once I got to my mother's, we packed a small bag of necessities and left for my Aunt Kalina's home. There it was, much the same, a bag and we left. We went to a hostel in the far west of town. A small no name place that took our cash and asked no questions about us. Lady Eirene's men were there within a day. We barely escaped with our lives and we have been on the run ever since. I would have kept running except my mother and aunt could not anymore. They are truly exhausted, and I brought them here as a last resort. They cannot go on like this."

"I understand. They and you will not need to go on like that any longer." I hesitate before asking this, but I need to hear the answer. "Valdís has told us some of what her life has been like and Pamphilos has shown us the letters you sent. I, I am hoping you will tell me that it was not as bad as I am hearing that it was."

She looks directly into my eyes and the pain reflected in hers tears my heart to shreds as she says, "It was so much worse than I could bring myself to write in those letters."

Valdís

I can't sleep. Knox is off doing whatever he does, and I am still so keyed up from dinner that I decide to walk through the gardens. They are in full bloom right now and the scents have calmed me some every time I have been out here. I brought my guards. They are trailing just a few steps behind me as I wander. Suddenly, a weirdly soft wall that smells amazing smacks into me. Arms go round me to stop me from falling when I am knocked back, electricity runs through my body as I recognize the scent of the man that has nearly run me down out here in the garden. Everything in my mind is screaming at me to run away from this man that has already made me cry once today, even if he was kind at dinner. I hear a low rumble in his chest and he says, "What have we here? A bunny in my gardens?"

Bunny! He thinks I am some small creature stealing from his fucking garden? Oh, fuck him. I try to push away from him, but the bastard isn't letting go. His hands stroke their way across my back till each gets to an arm as I fight the shiver trying to run through my body. He lets me step back a whole step before he asks, "What are you doing out here, Princess?"

This guy. "I was walking when some asshole nearly ran me down, not paying attention to where he was going. I would like to continue my walk, without said asshole, if you could see your way to getting your hands off me."

He chuckles, "I think I will keep my hands right where they are." His thumbs stroke my arms as he speaks, and it's all I can do not to sigh with pleasure at the touch. "I have news for you. Your Dagma is here."

My hands fly to his chest. "Here? Where? I need to go see her. You are going to let me see her, aren't you?"

He smiles and my heart melts. "Yes, but tonight she is very tired. She has been on the run since the morning you didn't come home. She is likely sleeping right now. But she knows you are here and you can have breakfast with her in the morning."

"Really?" I ask and when he nods yes, I am overjoyed that I will get to see my Dagma in the morning. I wrap my arms around him and hug him tight. "Thank you! I have missed her so much. Thank you!"

His arms slide around me slowly and I realize I am warm in the circle of his arms, that he is hugging me back. It feels really entirely too nice against his chest. The scent of him this close is setting me on fire and if the hardness I feel pressing into my belly is any indication, he is not unaffected. I ease back and he allows it until I try to step away. His hands grip my arms as he stares down at me. "Are you trying to run away, little bunny? Afraid of what the big bad wolf will do to you?"

"A little, since the big bad wolf seems to really dislike me and has a reputation for killing the people he doesn't like. Even if his scent does make me crazy."

He chuckles, and the sound sets off a flood in my pants. He inhales, "Ah, so it does. Knox said I needed to learn your scent so I would understand better. This is what you smell like when I am driving you crazy. It smells like I could drink you in and never tire of the taste." A small moan escapes my throat at the idea of his mouth on me. A low growl sounds in his throat, "You like that idea princess? The idea of my lips, my tongue tasting you. Nipping at your thighs, parting your lips so I could lap that nectar from the source?"

I am going to die if this man keeps talking, because I am going to attack him and ride him till I get my fill and he is going to kill me, but oh, what a way to go. I lift my eyes to look up at him as I raise my leg to run along his inner thigh slowly. His breath catches as mine comes faster. "I do like that idea, but only if you are still going to like me when it is done!" I drop my foot to the ground, stomping like a child, but his games are pissing me off. The shock in his eyes is kind of vindicating as I go on, "You are playing with me and I don't like it. I want you. There is no doubt about that. But I won't have you if you can't treat me like a person all the time. I don't care what you have going on, I got my own shit. If you want to have sex with me and no commitment beyond helping my people, I am so good with that. I could even maybe be persuaded if you wanted more. But nothing is happening until you aren't acting like you hate me on a regular basis. People that hurt my feelings and make me cry don't get to fuck me that same night. Now get your hands off me, please."

He is silent as he releases me. I step back and take a shaky breath because I am so horny I would fuck him for a stale dough round right now. "I hope that we can come to some sort of friendship or truce. I really do want you."

He nods and seems to be thinking as he says, "May I see you to your room?"

"Yes," I tell him as I turn back toward the castle, "I would very much like that." He steps up beside me and extends his arm in a silent offer. I take it and we walk toward the castle.

Nine

INGEMAR

Filing that suit was such a pain in the ass. Every single flunky with a clipboard needed the entire thing explained, and being charming for that long to people beneath me is the kind of drain only booze can fix. Which is why the tavern near the filing center has most of the cash I left with this morning. I am pouring another drink in my office when Hulthen taps on the door and enters saying, "I have a notice for you, sir, from the filing center."

I really didn't expect it to be that quick. They must be truly terrified. "Just set it on my desk Hulthen, I will read it shortly."

He does as I told him while I finish pouring. Walking over to my desk, I take a long pull from the glass before I sit down. Setting the glass carefully on my desk, I open the notice. It is, as I expected, a dismissal from the filing center. They say I should take this up directly with the kings; the center was not created for this sort of issue. Or that is the equivalent. Hulthen is back, tapping on my door again. He pops his head in and says, "Sir, there is a man here from the papers that would like to speak with you about your business at the filing center this morning."

Holy shit. That bitch was right. Fuck. "Send him in, Hulthen, and bring us both something light to eat. I haven't had my lunch just yet."

He nods and is quickly back with the man from the papers. He introduces himself but I don't care what his name is and I tell him, "Please, do sit. I have Hulthen bringing us some food. Would you care for a drink?"

He declines the drink and then Hulthen is there before he can ask his questions. Hulthen places plates next to each of us, asks if I require anything else and when I decline, he is gone.

The man from the papers jumps right into things. "Sir, I saw that you filed an interesting suit at the filing center this morning. Would you care to talk about that with me for the paper?"

I nod. "I would be delighted," I hold up the dismissal, "especially since it appears the morning was wasted."

The man smiles. "Nothing attempted is ever really wasted. After all, your story is going to go out to the entire island. Perhaps some good may yet come of it. Kings must serve their people after all and they too must maintain their reputations."

I pick at my food as I tell the man the sob story of how my son and heir Pelos had been intended for Valdís's husband since they were toddlers and that it was heartbreaking when we found out she wasn't entirely ok upstairs, if he knew what I meant. The man was near salivating as he took notes. I look forward to tomorrow's edition of the paper. It should be good.

He looks up from his notes. "Wasn't there something in the filing about an assault?"

I look away, as if embarrassed. "There was. It happened when the king came here, forced his way into my home, and kidnapped poor Valdís. She was screaming something awful as he dragged her from the house. Regrettably, there was nothing I could do, as I had already been knocked out by the king for daring to stand in the way of his prize. My son was still trying to help me stand as the king dragged the poor girl away."

"Is that what that bruise on your face is from?"

"It is. Maybe we could not focus on that for the story? What is important is they have Valdís and we must bring her safely home. Her mother is beside herself right now, what with her husband's recent death and the estate and the kidnapping. It is just so much for one widow. She has another daughter at home. She is terrified the kings will come for that one too."

"Oh really? And what was the family name?"

"Potentus. But I believe the widow Eirene would

prefer her solitude right now as she manages the estates. Perhaps give her some time, or set up an appointment?"

He nods. "Yes, we would want to respect the widow in her grief. I will send her a message today asking for an appointment."

We speak for a bit longer, but the man is antsy to leave and quickly makes his excuses to leave. When he is gone, I ring for Hulthen. He enters my office and I tell him to have this message delivered to Eirene now. Grabbing a sheet of paper I write, the first task is complete. Stuffing it in an envelope, I seal it and pass it to him. He leaves, envelope in hand, and walking fast to do my bidding.

Ten

KNOX

Waking up in my room this morning, I was more than a little concerned that perhaps everything had been a dream. Maybe Valdís was a figment of my imagination and the research I did late into the night was as well. I can't seem to shake the feeling, so I dress hurriedly and leave my room to go to hers. I will wake her and take her to breakfast. We can eat in the gardens. I really hated leaving her in her room alone last night, but I need to get to the bottom of where Eirene is descended from. I knock lightly on her door and wait a beat before I open it. She is very likely still asleep. The room is quiet and still dark when I enter, but I can hear her heart beating and it comforts me. Her scent, which fills this room, does something entirely else to me. I wonder how she feels about morning sex?

Only one way to find out. I make my way across the room to her bed and climb in. She is sleeping on her side and I lie next to her on the side she is facing. She is so lovely. I could watch her sleep for hours. I think maybe she would not appreciate that, so I run my fingers along her arm, brush her hair out of her face, just to try to gently alert her to my presence as I say, "Hello beautiful. Wake up, you gorgeous creature."

Her eyes open as I brush the hair away and I smile at her. She smiles back. "What time is it? Is it late? Have I missed breakfast?"

"No love, it is still early. Did you sleep well?"

"Sort of? It took me a long time to get to sleep because I was so excited about Dagma being here."

"Dagma is here?"

Her face crinkles as she asks, "Didn't Malic tell you?"

"No, I haven't seen him since dinner." I grin. "But you did I take it?"

"I did. I was walking in the gardens and," I must have had a look on my face because she interrupts herself with, "don't worry, my guards were with me. But anyway, he ran into me. We had a little argument, but then he told me about Dagma being here and said I could have break-fast with her this morning."

"That is wonderful. I am so happy your friend is here. What did you argue about?"

She blushes and her pheromones go into overdrive.

My cock notices as I breathe them in and gets hard, tenting my pants. Luckily, her eyesight is not as good as mine in the dark and she is unaware as she says, "Well, we were both rather excited at the physical contact. He kind of thought we would just do something about that. But I was still mad that he made me cry, and this was before he told me about Dagma, so I told him that I wouldn't be doing anything with someone that made me cry that day. He would have to treat me like a person before I would be willing to think about it."

I can't help myself. I start laughing. "What did he say?"

"Not much, actually. I think he was a little stunned that anyone would say no to him. Which I understand, I mean, you lot are kings. I can't imagine you hear no very often."

"I don't guess we do at that. Well, do I understand correctly that you ended up going to bed alone and unsatisfied?"

She smiles slowly, "You do."

"I could take care of that for you, if you would like," I tell her as I run the fingertips of one hand up from the curve of her hips to her shoulder and back down slowly.

She leans closer. "I would very much like that," she whispers, "but I have to pee first."

I laugh and roll onto my back, "I shall await your return right here, my lady."

She hops out of the bed and dashes across the room while I watch, happy to see that she is wearing a tiny slip of a nightgown and no panties. While she is gone, I shed clothing like a fiend.

When she comes back to the door, she says, "If I were to run and jump on top of you, could you catch me? With all that extra vampire strength you have?"

I look at her, excited by this prospect. "I don't even need vampire strength for this. You aren't as heavy as you think you are. Get over here."

She runs and leaps at me. I catch her around the waist easily and slowly lower her as she opens her legs to straddle me. My cock is ready for this and standing straight up. She reaches down and lines it up with her hole, moaning as she stretches around my cock. Her knees touch the bed and she takes control of the speed. Going so much slower, her hands on my chest as she impales herself. Fully impaled, she stops, her face a portrait of pleasure. It is all I can do to keep from lifting her and starting to rail the hell out of her, but I want to give her the opportunity to be in control. I watch her fucking fabulous round hips as she lifts herself, rolling her hips as she goes, and the feeling on my cock has me gripping the sheets and clenching my muscles to try to remain still as she does. She makes it up and down just a few times before I can't take it anymore. I lift her off of me and spin her around so she is facing the headboard as I get behind her growling, "Grab the headboard and hold on." She does as she's told for once and I fist my cock, lining it up with her entrance. I ease the head in and grab her hips, using them to hold her in place as I slam into her. I grit out, "Touch yourself. I am not going to last long."

She takes a hand from the headboard as I hold myself so very still as she gets her fingers to her clit and starts rubbing it hard and fast. Her pussy clenches around my cock and I cry out, "Oh, sweet Goddess! Valdís, you feel so fucking good. Come fast for me." I pull myself most of the way out of her and I start pounding her hard and fast. She is moaning and gasping, then I feel her pussy go wild as she shouts, "Oh fuck!" I fuck her harder and faster, coming just moments later, burying myself in her one last time to hold her close as we both recover.

A little later, we are curled up on our sides. Our breathing returned to normal and I ask her, "Are you ready to shower and go find breakfast?"

She chuckles. "I think I can walk to do that." Our shower is leisurely. I take the opportunity to wash her thoroughly. As I am washing her, she asks, "How is it you are able to survive so long without blood? I mean, you all need it to live, right?"

I nearly drop the cloth I am using to wash her when she asks that. "Yes, we do. Usually we drink when we are off Atlantis. We quit drinking from anyone here a long time ago. I guess I need to check on whether Malic brought any with him."

"Or you could drink from me."

I stand so quickly she nearly falls. I catch her by the upper arms and say, "Don't, don't say that."

She looks at me like I am an asshole for trying to protect her. "Well, how much do you drink?"

"Not a lot. Less than most women bleed in an hour when they menstruate."

Her eyes go wide. "Is that a possible source?" My cock springs up with a mind of its own about that as I try not to think about that mental picture. She is staring at my cock and looks up at me with a grin. "So you like that idea?"

I groan, "Well, yes. Mostly the part about licking your pussy."

"So, why not just drink from me?"

"I don't know? Because we don't drink from Atlanteans anymore?"

"Well, I want to try it. Besides, you need to eat and you should already be somewhere else, feasting. The least I could do is repay you with something I can easily replenish."

At this point in the steam perfumed with her scent, her arousal, her idea is sounding better and better. "Are you sure you want me to do this?"

She moves her hair back from her neck and tips her head to one side. "Bite me, big boy."

I can see the pulsing of a fresh supply. It is hypnotic, and I wrap my arms around her, lifting her up, bringing her neck closer to my mouth. I kiss the pulse point. It's racing now. Her legs are wrapped around me and I reach down to line my cock up with her entrance. She is soaked with more than just water. I graze her neck with my elongating teeth, ever so lightly. She shivers and her honey gushes onto my cock. Sinking my teeth into that tantalizing pulse of hers, I begin to drink as I lower her onto my cock. She moans and her pussy is quivering already. I drink slowly, fucking her with a slowness that has her squirming. I lock one arm around her waist to hold her and reach between us to rub her clit with my thumb. She comes on my cock with a scream, the pulsing, the gripping, wet heat of her pussy sends me over the edge and I come with her, drinking a few more little sips before I withdraw my teeth and lick her wounds to close them.

After we finish the rest of the shower, I dress in the bathroom and wrap a bath sheet around her. We walk into the bedroom together to find her something to wear. As we enter, I see Malic standing in the entry, "Hello Malic, unfortunately you missed the festivities, but doesn't she smell amazing fresh from the shower?"

His eyes narrow at me and I laugh as he says, "Valdís, I came to see if you would like to walk with me to have breakfast with Dagma and the two women she brought with her?"

She jumps into action and nearly drops the sheet as she says, "Yes! I'll be ready in just a minute!" She dashes into the closet and we can hear her shoving clothes on as fast as she can.

Ambling over to where Malic stands, I ask, "So how's that self control going Malic? Can you smell the sex we had? She felt amazing coming on my cock. You know, she wants you pretty bad. But I guess if you can't manage to be nice to her, I will just have to keep taking up the job you leave undone."

The last word is cut off as Malic's hand shoots out to grip my throat, "Fuck off, Knox. I don't need your shit right now."

Shoving his hand away, I laugh as Valdís comes out of the closet, stuffing her feet into shoes. "Just one more minute. I need to brush my hair before I see her."

Malic dips his head all friendly like at her saying, "Don't rush, take your time, breakfast won't start without you."

I can't resist messing with him. Mostly because having Valdís around has brought back my joy. Going through hundreds of years certain that you will never have a someone when you want the one you were told would be there so badly... It does something to a person. Or to a vampire. "She let me drink from her." His eyes fly to me. "In the shower. While I fucked her again. It was glorious."

His eyes narrow and he growls, "I'm warning you, Knox, I will bury you in a box under the castle. It will take you years to get back to the surface. Stop fucking with me. She did not."

A smirk on my face, I blow air at him. His nostrils flare, and I know he can smell her blood. He tackles me, saying, "How dare you drink from someone without their permission!"

I am laughing as Valdís comes running out of the bathroom shouting, "I asked him to do it! I asked him! I wouldn't take no for an answer. Don't hurt him over me!"

Malic is frozen, one fist pulled back and looking at her with sheer confusion on his face. "Why would you do that?"

She blushes furiously, but swallows and says, "I had an idea that it might feel really good. And I didn't want him to go hungry just because he chose to stay here with me. You know we can regenerate to make up for some blood loss, right?"

He looks down at me and I know he is going to hit me anyway, just seconds before his fist starts to move. I hear Valdís shouting as his fist crashes into my jaw. I laugh as he gets up and dusts himself off. She runs over to me. "Are you all right?" She turns back to him. "What the hell did you have to hit him for, anyway?"

He tugs on his sleeves as he carefully does not look at her. "For provoking me."

She giggles and looks back at me, "Man, are you bad at this. You aren't supposed to push them into punching you. The idea is kisses and sex."

I scowl at her, "I had kisses and sex, I was provoking him for the entertainment value. I simply misjudged where the line is." I grin up at him. "I didn't realize he was that long without."

Malic glares at me. "Under the palace, Knox. Under the palace."

Valdís shakes her head at the both of us. "Ok then. I am ready to go to breakfast. Where are we going, Malic?"

He extends a hand to help her up off the floor and then puts his arm around her to guide her as he says, "I picked a nice spot in the gardens and I have plenty of men patrolling to ensure we are not disturbed by any unwanted guests."

I get up off the floor and follow them. She looks back at me, eyes wide and mouths, "Is he okay?"

I smile and nod as I walk behind them. She doesn't look entirely reassured as she turns around.

Malic

I knew he drank from her. He doesn't know I was watching. Or that I came watching them fuck while he drank from her. Neither of them does. And they won't if I have anything to do with it. I was cleaned up and waiting for them when they came out of the bathroom. She looked less surprised than I thought when they walked out of the bathroom, but no way she saw me. Her eyes were closed.

When he drank from her, the scent of her blood perfuming the air nearly did me in. Seeing her face as she came did do me in. I came in my hand, watching her and hearing her scream as she came on his cock while he drank from her.

I hate how weak I am over her. What if she dies too because I am too weak to stop it from happening? How can I be strong enough to protect everyone when all I want to do anymore is drop to my knees and worship at the join of her thighs?

Knox catches up and takes her other arm, the three of us walking together down the hall to find Dagma and company in the gardens. It feels so good, so right. But it makes me so weak, I can't let myself succumb to this need.

Eleven

Eirene

I am celebrating in my office when my darling daughter comes to see me, "My sweet Eumeleia, come sit, let me pour you some honeyed wine, we will drink to success together."

She is quiet and noticeably less than celebratory as I pour her wine. She must still have a crush on that wretched trash Pelos. If she only knew how truly awful he is. I kept tabs on that boy and I know how many servants he has gone through, whether he killed them or they died because of him. The result is the same. And that doesn't begin to touch on how the sex workers won't go anywhere near him for any amount of money. Not even his father can buy him a piece of ass. Which is exactly why he is perfect for Valdís, not my sweet Eumeleia. She will understand in time. Turning back to her with our drinks in hand, I see her staring at a picture of her father with that look on her face.

I manage to stop my eyes from rolling as her father also knew what kind of person Pelos is and was quite determined that neither of his daughters would ever be part of that family. "Here you go, my darling, have a drink. Celebrate with me." as I cross the room to her, she schools her features into something more acceptable than the longing with which she stared at that picture.

She accepts the drink and smiles, "What are we celebrating?"

"Plans coming together, of course! The plan to discredit all the kings is starting to work. Have we gotten the rsvp's back from the ladies for my tea? I can't very well reenter society if they don't go along with it. I am hoping the curiosity about the current situation will draw them, if nothing else."

"The rsvp's have all been returned and everyone accepted. Well," she pauses, looking into her glass, "Pelos' mother won't be attending. She is not doing well and isn't able to go out."

I'm sure that is a huge surprise for her husband. "What a shame! We'll send her our regards and perhaps a basket."

She looks up at me, "Mom, our families have always been close. Maybe we should pay a visit to them in their time of need."

"Oh darling," I turn to go seat myself behind the desk,

"the poor woman is ill. We can't traipse over there and bring in our germs while she is so weak. We'll wait until she is well and go visit her. Talk about her miraculous recovery." Or we'll dress in black and attend her funeral while lamenting how young she was when she took ill and died so suddenly.

A knock sounds on my door and Flavi peeks in. "Mistress, the papers have come in. You said you wanted to see them immediately?"

"Yes! Bring them in! Thank you Flavi!" She scurries across the room and sets them on the desk before me, with a quick curtsy, and she is heading back out the door.

Setting my glass down, I pick up the first one and I am thrilled to see an article about the kings assaulting Ingemar and kidnapping my daughter. This is perfect! It is a splash piece. They embellished everything. The kings look horrible. All of society will see this before my tea and be eager to ask questions.

Everything is coming together perfectly.

Twelve

VALDÍS

I cannot believe my life right now. I haven't managed to do any of what I came here to do. I feel completely useless. At the same time, I am having kind of depraved sex with one of the kings escorting me right now. Worse yet, the other one watched. I don't know if that makes it more depraved or not. I think probably yes because as soon as I smelled Malic; I was even more turned on than I already was. Now I am being escorted by both of them and I just want to drag them onto me. I don't care if it is a dark corner or the entire guard watches. My need is that big.

The only thing stopping me is that we are on our way to see my Dagma. I have missed her so much and worried that my mother may have killed her by now with as long as I have been gone. Now I have to wonder how bad has it been that she overcame her fears of the kings and came here for shelter.

We reach the gardens and a little way in; I see my Dagma sitting at a table. Removing my arms from the king's arms, I run to my Dagma. She turns and her face lights up when she sees me barreling toward her. Skidding to a stop, I drop to my knees before her and throw my arms around her. She gathers me into her arms, resting my head on her shoulder, "Oh child, I have missed you. And worried so much! When you didn't come back that night, with all the commotion that went on, I feared the worst. Until Lord Ingemar stole you away and good King Knox came to get you," She must have felt me tense at the idea she could have still been at mother's then. "Don't worry, I had long been on the run by the time that happened. I just have friends in many places and they get word to me about the ones I care about." She puts her hands on my arms and pushes me gently back. "You should eat. Come sit next to me and we will eat together like we did when you were little."

I chuckle as I get to my feet. "I don't think we need to worry so much about the food being tainted here."

Dagma laughs, "No, I don't suppose we do. And isn't that a relief? Gentlemen, will you be dining with us, or did you plan to hover like gargoyles with crowns?"

Knox laughs out loud and starts walking over from where they had stopped at the edge of the clearing. Malic is slower to move, an obstinate set to his lips as he starts to move. "We don't wear crowns to breakfast."

Dagma bobs her head, "Pardon me your majesty, it was more a figure of speech than an observation of facts," She watches as Knox starts to take the seat next to me, looks at Malic and moves over one, leaving only the seat next to me he seats himself with a grin. I can only imagine that is because he must have known that Malic was watching, that we were not the only ones coming right then. I feel my cheeks heat and I look down at the empty plate in front of me. Dagma suddenly says, "Valdís, I want to introduce you to my mother, Katrina." She gestures toward the woman next to her and then toward the woman sitting on the other side of her mother. "This is my aunt Kalina."

"Very nice to meet you both. I'm so sorry that it is under such poor circumstance."

The two older women laugh and Kalina says, "Aside from the exhaustion, this has been the most excitement we have had in years. Plus, now we are in the palace! Dining with kings, how often does this happen?"

Katrina nods, but is more reserved than Kalina, saying only, "It is a change. I think it might be good."

I see a mostly healed bruise on Dagma's face and ask, "Did she do that to you?"

Dagma nods. "I wasn't quite fast enough getting Quorin out, so I let her find me instead of Quorin. She didn't hit me much, and it's nearly gone. I won't be going back to work for her again, so it doesn't matter."

"It does matter. She shouldn't be so terrible to you. You've done nothing but try to protect me. Then again, perhaps that is sin enough in her eyes."

Dagma looks away. "Yes, I think it was." She takes a breath and turns back. "But it's nothing to worry ourselves with now. The kings have us all here. I am sure everything will be straightened out soon enough and we can go home. Let the kings get back to their lives." I cut my eyes to glance at Knox and Malic under my lashes. Neither looks thrilled with that plan. Well, we'll burn that bridge when we get to it. Dagma begins telling stories about my childhood. They revolve mostly around time with my father. I listen to them, mostly forgetting to eat with my chin on my hands, watching the memories play in my mind.

Then Malic says, "Her father was a good man. But this leaves me with questions. Your stories show how much he seemed to love Valdís. So why did the father that loved her so much but did nothing all these years to stop the abuse, suddenly leave the estate to her? He had to know her mother would fight her about it. It is very strange and we are going to look into the reasons for this."

Dagma bites her lip. "I think I can answer that question." Both kings look at her and so do I, because I really want to know the answer to this. Wringing her hands, she says, "Valdís, when your parents were first trying to conceive, they had a really hard time. Nothing was working. So they finally go to the doctor and he tells them that their bodies are not compatible with creating life."

I gasp, "How horrible that must have been for them!" Then my brain kicks in. "But if that is true, how did my sister and I come about? Are we adopted?"

Dagma grimaces. "Not exactly. See, Eirene wanted a child badly. She was willing to do anything to have one as a child would cement her position in her social group, as they were all having babies then. The doctor told them that Eirene would not be able to have a child by anyone from this island. Your father, bless him, told her it would be fine if they never had children. Eirene refused to accept that. She told your father that she didn't care how it happened. She better have a babe in her arms. It wasn't very long before she came around asking me about my relationships or lack of really, and how I felt about having children. Was my family fertile? That sort of thing. Since none of us really can have a bunch of children, but my family pretty reliably had at least one child." A suspicion is forming in my mind as I listen to her tell the story. It can't be. It just isn't possible. "The very afternoon she was asking all those questions I am cleaning in one of the upstairs bedrooms and she drags your father in, telling him that he is to impregnate me and they would take the child and raise it as theirs."

"Oh my Goddess, are you saying you and my father, that I'm your daughter?"

Wringing her hands and biting her lip as she looks hard at her lap, she says, "Yes. Though I am not listed on the record. If they tested your blood against hers, they wouldn't find any of her in you. Are you very upset?"

Katrina speaks then, "I can't speak for her, but I damn well am. You mean I have had a granddaughter all this time, and you never told me?"

Tears run hot from the corners of my eyes. "Goddess, no, I am not upset with you. I mean, it would have been nice to know. Instead of growing up thinking, my mother hated me. But she's just my stepmother and my mother was there protecting me the whole time. Oh Dagma, I am not upset at all. If anything, I wish I could have known before now."

Knox is the one that asks, "Did you give birth to Eumeleia as well?"

I wipe away my tears as Dagma, mom, sniffles into a tissue Katrina produced. She looks up at us and says, "No. I didn't. When Valdís was just a few months old, Eirene announced at dinner one night that a miracle had happened and she was pregnant. Your father was horrified because at that point, she had already tried to murder you. He dragged her from the room and demanded an explanation. It is shameful to admit, but I listened at the door. He was demanding to know how she made this happen when he hadn't touched her since the first time she tried to murder little Valdís. She screamed at him that she found a real man to do what he couldn't do and he should just be glad. Told him that two children would merely prove how virile he was. They fought for quite some time. Eirene never did give up a name that I know."

"Holy shit. So the only people in that house that I am related to are Dad and you." Realization dawns, "And Lommán! I have a brother? Half brother? Is he my father's son as well?"

"No," Dagma chuckles, "Your father and I weren't lovers. We didn't actually... hm, oh this. I never expected to need to explain this. We didn't touch to create you. Which is why we thought it meant to be. Your father gave me a large syringe filled with his seed. I went to my room and, um, injected it. I laid there for a while to try to keep it in there. I must have fallen asleep, though. Suddenly I heard a woman's voice saying it is done. I opened my eyes, but there was no one there, of course. After Eirene came up pregnant, your father told me he wrote every-thing down. Even things I didn't know about. He said it was written down and hidden where no one would ever find it. If he disappeared, you would be able to find them in the barn. He said you would need them and that perhaps you would remember the working of the latch so the entire floor of his office out there would not have to be torn up." She looks directly at Malic and Knox. "I feel certain the reason that he wanted his estate to go to Valdís is so that it would remain in Atlantean hands. He said Eirene couldn't be Atlantean, it just wasn't possible."

Ingemar

The crowd here is a lot bigger than I expected. The papers have done my job for me and I didn't even have to pay them for it. Pelos is so excited he is having problems keeping calm. That boy is too much like his mother. I need to have Hulthen get out my mourning clothes. I think the boy's mother is only going to last maybe another week, less if I give her an extra dose.

Ah yes, Lord Judda is just wrapping up. My time to shine. Lord Judda calls me up to the podium, the people cheer as I take the space he vacated. Pelos stands next to me, managing to look suitably sad for all that his latest favorite is in the front row.

"I know it is a difficult thing to believe that the ones entrusted so long ago with protecting us would turn on us. And I don't believe they have. They are tired and misunderstood and have had the pressure of ruling for far too long. No person or persons were meant to be in charge of our little continent, barely big enough to escape being called an island, for so very long. But they have done it. They haven't had the time to change, they have a way of doing things and that is it. They are still operating from an ancient worldview. Which is why when they real-ized that poor Valdís had gone home to be wed they responded the way barbarians would, with violence.

I don't condone what they did but I understand where it came from. And really, Pelos and I, we just want our

Valdís back home, safe and happy with her new family. We want to take care of our sweet but confused girl. Her poor mother is even more worried, but with the recent death of her husband, she hadn't even had time to mourn when Valdís went missing. We both still have our questions as to how that happened. However, none of it will matter if we can just get my soon to be daughter back safe. Thank you all for your support, I can only hope the kings will hear our pleas and be moved to act in a way that displays their humanity."

I step back and allow Pelos to add his well planned thoughts to the matter for the crowd. As he regurgitates the speech I made him practice until he could recite it backwards I study the crowd. Women are crying, husbands and fathers look angry. Sons around marrying age appear ready to fight for Valdís's honor. This is going so much better than I could have imagined.

Pelos wraps his plea for his future bride to be let to come home and the crowd cheers, it's like thunder rolling down the mountain. There is no way the kings will be able to ignore this.

Thirteen

"The time is now Eirene."

I hear his voice as I enter my bedchamber and my eyes go directly to the small plant sitting on the side table. "Thy will be done," I reply as I collect the plant and head back out of my room. I meet Flavi on the way and tell her to get someone to the car to drive me. She races off to carry out my orders as I continue on at a pace more becoming of a lady. The plant is light and filled with thorns. It looks almost like the plant Crown of Thorns, but modified. If I am understanding correctly, it will be poison to anyone attempting to get rid of it. Or fight it off.

A driver is waiting when I get to the car. He opens the door for me, asking, "Where shall I take you tonight, ma'am?"

"About halfway up the road to the palace. Can you do that?"

"I'll do my best. Are we in a hurry or would you like me to drive slow?"

"Don't dawdle, but don't draw attention."

"Yes ma'am," he says as he closes the door behind me while I settle into my seat. The drive up is relatively quick and completely uneventful. We get to the spot and I tell him, "turn the car around, but then stop and wait while I attend to my business."

"Yes, ma'am."

He has the car turned around quickly and when he stops; he puts the car in park and hops out to open my door for me. I hand him the plant first and then ease myself out of the car. "Wait in the car for me."

He nods and I walk off to the side of the road. Finding a likely spot, I pull the trowel out of my pocket and dig a hole just larger than the pot. Minutes later, I have the plant in its new space in the ground and I must read the lines to unlock its powers:

Crowns and Thorns
    You we scorn
    In castle you'll stay
    My poison plant blocking the way
    For every cut, three more vines grow
    Surrounding the castle, none of it for show
    In and around,

Twisted and bound
No more are you free
For you will cease to be

While I was thankful for the bright moonlight that allowed me to see the words, now... I watch as the plant begins to grow at an alarming rate and I hurry to get in the car and tell my stupid driver to get going. He starts us back toward the house as I turn round in my seat to watch out the back window as the plant covers the roadway on its way to circle the castle.

Ingemar

It isn't long after the rally and the motivation of the crowd approval that the other lords come to pay me a visit. Hulthen shows them into my office and I arrive moments later, making sure to look as though I have attempted to be properly attired but not quite succeeded.

Stepping into the office, I put my head down and close the door behind me, slumping on it just briefly before someone clears their throat. A small jerk upright and a greeting, "Gentlemen, my apologies. I did not realize you had already been shown in. It's so hard to find good help these days."

They nod, sympathy plain on their faces. Lord Judda asks, "How is your wife today?"

I walk across the room to sit behind my desk. "She is not well, gentlemen. Not well at all. She has always been somewhat a fragile creature. And now I, I fear the stress of this may kill her." They make the appropriate noises of concern and I say to them, "But enough of my problems. What can I do for you today, gentlemen?"

They exchange looks and nods before Lord Judda turns back to me saying, "Lord Ingemar, we have been discussing this kidnapping business and to a man, all agree it is a sorry business. And it is just indicative of how the kings have slipped further and further into their more base natures over time. We think it is time for a new ruler, a single king, as opposed to the five that are left of the original set." He looks hard at me and I raise my chin a fraction, "we have decided that you should be the next king. You are one of us and know the proper way of doing things. You have been directly affected by this latest debacle with the kidnapping, and you have shown real leadership in trying to hold the kings accountable for their actions."

Widening my eyes a bit and letting my jaw drop, I say, "Gentlemen, I don't know what to say. I certainly wasn't expecting this," I look down at my lap to keep from laughing at how serious they all are, "to happen. I don't quite know what to say."

Lord Judda bobs his head. "I understand, but the fact is we need new leadership and you are the only one we are all in agreement to back. And we have a tentative idea about how to put this into motion."

Now I am actually surprised. What do these idiots have planned? "You have a plan?"

He bobs his head again, for all the world looking like a well-pleased turkey. "We do! But first, before we discuss plans or strategies or anything else, what is your decision? Will you become king or back down like some coward before their might?"

I nearly laugh but manage to make it look like a slow smile spreading across my face. "Gentlemen, you've got yourself a king. With you all as my advisors, how could I go wrong?"

They cheer and I get some wine from my stash, pouring glasses for everyone. Once we are all toasted and settled, I bring them back to what I wanted to know to begin with, "What are these tentative plans you all have made?"

Lord Judda says, "We want to create a small army of assassins. We'll send them up to pick off the king in place, King Knox. After that, we just assign people we trust to wait for the others to wake up at their assigned time. When they emerge, they die. It's a simple plan, and keeping things simple is the best way I know to stop them going awry."

Sipping my wine to buy time, I mull it over. It really

isn't a terrible plan. "Where are you going to find your small army of assassins?"

"There are small enclaves throughout the continent, small as it is, where one can find those types of people. I dare say Valdís' mother could tell you where to find the local chapter, as I believe they did a job for her not long ago."

I hide my surprise. I had no idea. But that is good to know. It will definitely help me later. "And how do we plan to collect them?"

Lord Judda chuckles, "Many of us are long overdue for visiting family in different parts of the continent. Now seems like an opportune time to pay short visits to see loved ones we have ignored for much too long."

"I like it. When do we start?"

"We will begin to slowly trickle in and out-of-town tomorrow. Our new hires will come to town slower and bunk with us until they are all arrived, at which time we can move forward with things."

We are up late into the night discussing how we will take over the kingdom. Not a single one of these fools suspecting that they are doing exactly as I wanted them to do. Exactly as I set them up to decide upon. Eirene has no idea and won't until it is too late. By the time she figures it all out, she will be dying and her daughter will be my new prize. I can't wait to take her. Those luscious curves have haunted me since I had her in my grasp for that short time. When I get her, I will never let her go.

Fourteen

VALDÍS

The gardens have become my refuge when I need space and grounding. My guards pick their spots and after a bit I can pretend they aren't there. It is silence and solace and I feel at peace in these gardens in a way I have never felt anywhere else. I wonder if they would let me visit when I can finally go home? I mean, I would miss them deeply, but in a weird way I think this garden would be where my real sorrow lay, I wonder why that is? Because home was something I never felt? Even when I was with my father, he was great but all the times he didn't protect me from her... Why didn't he make her stop? That should have been something well within his power to do.

A scent drifts my way on the breeze, Malic. I tell my guard; the king is coming. They seem to melt further into the darkness. If I didn't know where they were, I would swear I was alone. Malic strides into the little clearing and skids to a stop. "What are you doing out here? And especially what the fuck are you doing out here alone?"

The growl in his voice as he said the last part sent shivers down my spine and heat spiking in all the right places. Or they would be the right places if he was interested in me that way. "I am not alone. My guards backed away a bit when I told them you were coming. I thought that would be best since you probably would not want an audience, no matter how much you enjoy watching yourself."

His eyes narrow. "I don't know what you're talking about."

I raise an eyebrow. "Really? Would you like me to describe it to you? Tell you how I was showering with Knox. How I convinced him to drink from me while he fucks me. How your scent wafted in and turned me on even more? How my eyes opened just enough for me to see you—"

"No! That's enough!" He drags a hand across his face, but that doesn't hide the bulge in his pants or how he leaned my way a little.

He looks angry now, and I have this insane urge to poke the bear. Standing, I stalk toward him, "Why are you mad? Because I knew you were there? Or maybe the way Knox filled my pussy while drinking from my neck bothers you more? Perhaps you are just disgusted that it was me at all? Mad because you think that I am desecrating the kingdom, spreading these thick thighs for Knox?"

His hands shoot out and grab my arms, snatching me up against him and kissing me hard. His lips punishing mine till I open to him and he ravishes my mouth as my hands hold on to his jacket for all I am worth. His cock is pressing into me as he breaks the kiss off, leaving us both gasping for air. He presses me harder against him for just a moment before he sets me carefully away from him. "I am mad it wasn't me. Mad that I wanted it to be me. Mad that it is a weakness inherent in me that could get the people that have been my brothers for so long hurt. Maybe dead. And what if I cared for you? You are even less capable of defending yourself than they were. You are so fragile that I probably bruised you just now! You would be a weakness for anyone to exploit!"

He begins to pace back and forth, his hands clenching over and over again. I feel such pain in my heart for this man who closed himself off so much that even the idea of caring for someone does this to him. I feel the hot tears tracking down my face and tip my chin up, anyway. "Caring for people is never a weakness, it only makes you stronger."

He spins and stomps over to get in my face. "And when they die? When you lose them to murdering savages that think they are so advanced? When they are dead and gone, then what? When it was your job to protect them? Does that make you stronger?"

"It can. Or it can make you so scared of the pain of

losing someone that you wall yourself off in fear and pain from everyone and everything. I can't promise that I won't die. In fact, with as many people as want me dead, as many times as I have already escaped attempts on my life, it is pretty likely I will be dead soon. But I am here now. We can have this moment. Maybe we can have a few more before someone manages to kill me."

His eyes squeeze shut, and he tips his head back. Looking as though he is silently screaming at the sky as he drops to his knees before me. He opens his eyes. "How can you bear it? The loss of people? The knowing that you will lose them? How are you so calm in the face of your own death?"

He is slumped now, his chin near resting on his chest as he sits before me. Stepping forward, I put a finger under his chin, gently guiding him to look at me. "I love them as much as I can while I have them. I remember them well when they are gone. That's really all we can do."

His arms are suddenly around my waist as he crushes me to him, his hot tears soaking my shirt. My arms go round him of their own accord and I stroke his head while he cries. Eventually his tears dry and his arms aren't crushing me anymore when he murmurs, "You smell so fucking good. You smell better than anything I have ever smelled. It took every ounce of willpower I possess to not hunt down the source of your scent when I first got home."

Chuckling, I say, "Yeah, that's kind of how you all smell to me, too."

He presses his face into my belly as he breathes in my scent. I feel a flood of moisture and heat in my pussy that I am trying really hard to ignore when he says, "How do you stand it? How can you stand being around us and smelling this scent all the time without," he nips my belly through my clothing and my knees nearly give out. Fuck! I didn't even have a clue I would like being bitten there! "Biting someone or attacking us?"

"A ton of restraint and sometimes excusing myself from the room."

He flinches and pulls back a little to look up at me. "I am so sorry about that. It didn't occur to me that you wanted me as bad as I wanted you. I thought—it doesn't matter what I thought. I was wrong and I apologize." His hands are on my hips now, mine on his massive shoulders. My core is throbbing with desire as his thumbs start moving up and down. My eyes close and my head tips back a little as I just enjoy the sensation. His fingers splay and his thumbs press in a little more. I feel his thumbs catch the bottom edge of my shirt and lift, the cool breeze hitting my belly just before his tongue. He groans, in pleasure or pain I don't know, but his tongue is like electricity on my body and I want nothing more than for him to keep touching, keep licking me. He sucks gently on my belly as his hands move to push my shirt up further. The need pouring through me to mate this man is so strong. I don't understand how I didn't recognize that this is what happened with Knox. I was mating with him. Holy shit. Maybe I should stop him. Then his thumbs brush the underside of my breasts.

My nipples tighten into hard peaks, just begging for his mouth to cover them. He kisses and nips his way up. My body is on fire for him. He growls, "How attached are you to these clothes?"

I come down a little from the place outside time where I was enjoying all the touch when he repeats the question. "Oh, um, you all provided these. I guess ask Epaphras?"

He snarls at me, "Why would I ask Epaphras? Are you sleeping with him?"

"What? No! Jeez. He is the one that puts the clothes in my closet. I have no idea where they come from beyond that. I care nothing about them. Stop asking me about stupid shit. Put your mouth back where it belongs!"

One side of his mouth lifts in a sexy grin as his hands move to the center of my shirt. I watch as he holds it taut and his nails grow sharp and extend, pressing through the cloth like it was nothing. He grasps the fabric and one swift tug has it in two pieces, the lace bra underneath no protection from the breeze or his eyes feasting on their prize. He drops the edges of my shirt and I work to pull the remains of it off my body. He pulls the cups of my bra under my breasts, so gently, no trace of the nails that just tore through my shirt. My nipples are so tight they hurt until he puts his mouth on one and a sigh escapes my lips.

My hands twine in his hair. I want him to never stop. He lets go, opens his mouth and starts to withdraw. I whimper in need. He chuckles, "Don't worry princess, I won't leave you in need again." And he moves to the other breast, lips closing around my nipple as he suckles while running his tongue over it and around it, making me moan with the pleasure of it.

I feel one of his hands tug on the waist of my pants briefly, but before I can move, I feel them falling away. His hand goes around the back of my calf and slowly moves up my leg to stop, cupping my ass. When he starts kissing and licking his way down my body, I don't know whether to groan in frustration at the lack of attention on my breasts or moan in anticipation of where he might be going. He presses a kiss on my mound, then lifts one of my legs and puts it over his shoulder. The hand still on my ass keeps me from landing on said ass. When his tongue licks up the center of my pussy, the hands that were flailing about go straight back to his hair and hold on for dear life. He uses that tongue like I am a delicacy to be savored and alternates it with trying to suck my soul out through my clit. Then he does both at the same time, and I sail right over the edge, shattering into a million pieces in his mouth. He pulls away, and even that movement triggers spasms in my body. I realize as he repositions his hands and moves my leg off his shoulder that he has been holding me up. Sweet Lady, I love a strong man. Just as I start to get my feet under me, he stands and lifts me off the ground entirely. I yelp and wrap my legs around his waist. My hands never left his hair. He keeps one arm around my waist, holding me up as he reaches under me with the other. As he lowers me and I feel him line his cock up with my entrance, I am a little surprised by the girth. The head feels huge. He lowers me so slowly, the stretch of it is amazing. I want him to get it in, but I want to feel this stretch forever. The head is fully in and the rest isn't any smaller, or at least it doesn't feel like it is. But it feels so good, like everything in me was waiting for the moment I would join with this man. My eyes roll back and close as the torment of pleasure continues. I feel his body fully against mine as he says, "Open your eyes princess, I want to see you when I come."

My eyes fly open at that and his eyes are glowing, fangs bared. It's so fucking sexy my core clenches around his cock, making him moan a little as I ask, "Will you bite me? Will you feed from me as you fuck me too?"

The flash in his eyes as he says, "Yes! Tasting you with my cock buried in you is all I could want and more!"

I should be afraid as this fanged monster descends upon the throat I have so willingly offered up. I'm not though. For all that they are the monsters I have never felt so safe as I do with them. His teeth pinch and pleasure explodes in my body as he bites down while he starts to fuck me. One arm around my waist and the other buried in my hair as he drinks his fill and fucks me into oblivion.

When I am able to comprehend the world around me again, I realize he didn't even take off his clothing for this. Not only that, he has a couple drops of blood on his shirt. He is setting me gently on my feet, his cock is still hard though I felt him come. I should probably have a talk with these guys about the birds and the bees. I don't think they want me pregnant any time ever, but they are not cautious at all. Maybe because our people are not terribly fertile? I don't know. I mean, I wouldn't be mad. It would definitely mean no one would ever want to marry me... You know... No. I should have the talk with them. Just in case. It's not right for any of us to ignore this possibility. Once he is sure I am stable, Malic lets me stand on my own as he shrugs off his jacket and holds it out for me to put my arms through. I do and the jacket is warm as it swallows me. It's a surprisingly nice feeling, his jacket enveloping my body like this.

He offers his arm to me and I say, "Shouldn't we pick up my clothes? Let me just get them. There has to be a bin on the way." He shrugs as if to say suit yourself. I grab them and ball them up. I tuck them against me as I step over to take his arm. As I do, he takes the clothing from me and carries it himself. I hear my guards fall in behind us as we head for the castle. I am slightly embarrassed that they were there for that, but it's also weirdly hot to know that at the very least, they were all listening. Going to have to try real hard not to dwell on that little bit later, especially when I have to talk to them.

Looking up at Malic, I decide to go ahead and leap

into the hard stuff. I think any guy willing to cry on me can deal with this conversation. "I noticed that, um, you didn't pull out or anything. And it occurred to me that Knox doesn't either. Are you all aware that it is possible to get a woman pregnant? I mean, I am not worried about it at all. Having a baby would be great and it would make me not at all marriage material for anyone. That would be great. No more idiot suitors. Probably even Pelos would leave me be at that point."

Malic stops and turns me to face him with his faster than light hands suddenly appearing on my shoulders. I am looking up at him when he says, "First, you are off the market. No one is marrying you unless it is one of us. Period. Second, if you were to fall pregnant with a child of ours, well, nothing would make us happier. Not only would it be a joyous event in itself, it would be yet another proof that Knox is right and you are the one."

"You know, Knox made mention of something like that, but said he wants to wait and explain later. It would be great if you all could get with the sharing. Why is a pregnancy a proof of anything beyond sex?"

He slips my arm in his again and we start walking again. "Because none of us are compatible with anyone else. No one else on or off this planet can fall pregnant from sex with us unless they are the one."

Two of the guards dart ahead of us to open and hold the doors as we walk in. I whisper a thank you to the one nearest me and get the barest of nods in return. I am thrilled at the acknowledgement. As we near the hall that is the king's wing, I see Knox coming our way. He grins at my attire and as he gets closer, he says, "Valdís, what a nice jacket you have there. Care to share what clothing you have left under there?" I glance around. The only person in front of me is Knox. The guards behind me, well, this isn't the most they could have seen tonight. I open the jacket to reveal my body, naked but for the lace bra, cups still tucked under my breasts. Knox groans, "Damn it, woman, I didn't think you really would."

Closing the jacket, I tell him, "I'm feeling like granting wishes tonight."

He takes the few steps that bring him to stand before me and kneels. Taking the hand holding the jacket closed, he says, "Dear lady, grant my wish and let me share your bed tonight. Let me feast upon the sweet center at the juncture of your thighs until you scream my name."

Malic snorts as I exhale a shaky breath. "Um, yes. Oh, my. Definitely yes."

Malic takes his arm from mine and fists his hand in my hair, turning me toward him as he tips my head back. "And will you let me join you in your bed tonight as well? Will you take us both tonight?"

My eyes are so wide they feel a little dry like my throat, guessing that is because all the liquid in my body just went to my pussy. I swallow and answer the only way I possibly can. "Yes." These two men may not know it, but they are part of my very soul now. There is nothing they could ask that I wouldn't do for them, except to leave.

Knox breathes in deeply, "Fuck. That made her so hot for us. We need to get to that room now or we are doing this right here in the hall."

Malic lets go of my hair and scoops me up into his arms, striding through the castle toward my room.

Before I know it, we are in my bedroom, in the middle of that huge bed. The bed Knox said was meant for thirteen, but tonight will hold the two kings I am irrevocably tied to by bonds stronger than I could ever have imagined. Malic is before me, kissing me like he'll never stop as his hands roam my body. Knox is behind me, nibbling my neck, where their hands meet as they roam my body. They don't shy away from each other, their hands roam each other too. I don't know what to focus on. My mind is spinning in a haze of love. Love? Oh, no... I love these men? What was I thinking? Being connected is one thing, but love, they could hurt me with that. How did I not realize these bonds would include love? And suddenly all thought flies from my mind as I feel hands, fingers, at my front and back entrances. Oh sweet lady, the things they are doing with their hands feel amazing. I don't know what hand belongs to who and I don't care. I feel fingers enter me from both sides, slowly and well oiled. Where did they find, a thumb presses my clit just right and I am coming all over someone's hand. The hands slowly exit me, the pleasure nearly too intense.

Malic lifts me and falls back on the bed, gently setting me on top of him. I lift a little and his cock is at my entrance immediately. I feel Knox's fingers caressing my pussy as I sink onto Malic's cock. Malic's hands are on my hips as I start to ride him and Knox's fingers slip in with it. Another finger from somewhere is rubbing my clit and I wonder if I can die of pleasure? The fingers leave my pussy and I swear I feel Knox's cock easing into me as I slowly ride Malic and, oh fuck me, it is. Two cocks, how is that fitting in me? How does it feel so fucking good? I'm not even moving any more, they are holding me up and touching me while they fuck me in perfect rhythm. My orgasm hits me like a freight train. I feel it in my entire body. Then I feel them coming, both slamming into me to hold themselves in place. It sets off a whole new wave of convulsions. As I start to return to my body, I feel two cords snap into place. It feels like nothing I have ever felt before. Like, this is where I belong. I feel the tears on my face and I don't care. For once, I am not afraid of the tears. Or what will happen if they see them. Knox pulls out gently and heads for the bathroom. Malic rolls me onto my side and pulls out. He reaches up and brushes my hair away from my face. My knee is lifted and my legs spread. I look down just as Knox places a warm cloth on my pussy, cleaning the mess of their seed from me.

I've never had such considerate men, ever. Much less two. Knox takes the soiled cloth back to the bathroom as Malic tugs the blankets down so he can cover me with them. Knox climbs back in the bed, slipping under the covers and cuddling up to my back even as Malic cuddles me from the front. Their arms cross me to rest their hands on each other. If this is what love is like, I could maybe be all right with this.

Malic

I wake slowly, enjoying the feel of waking next to someone. A feeling I thought I would never have again. I open my eyes slowly and angle my head to watch her sleep. Knox is right. I could no more deny that she is our queen than I could will myself to stop living. No one but our queen would be able to find the heart of me so quickly and rip out the parts that have been festering since the deaths of our brothers, leaving me able to finally start the healing so long overdue. Valdís opens her eyes and stares directly at me. "Why were you looking for me in the gardens?"

"What? How do you know I was looking for you in the gardens?"

She scowls at my non-answer. "The lady in my dream told me."

My soul freezes in place. She can't mean what I think she means. "What lady?"

Valdís shrugs, "I don't know. She didn't exactly introduce herself. She said you would know who she is, but she's not talking to you just yet. You aren't ready for that. She told me you were looking for me and I should ask you why. It is important. She also said you were watching me sleep and if I woke up right then I would catch you at it. You know that's a little weird, right? So why were you looking for me?"

"I. Um. Well." The Goddess can't be talking to her in her dreams. She can't be. "I was going to tell you that we will be sending someone to your home to collect your father's journals."

Valdís bolts upright in the bed. "You can't! You won't be able to find them without destroying them! I know where they are, and I know the traps he set. If you open it the wrong way, we lose everything. I have to be there. You can't send someone else to get them."

I sit up slowly. "We can and we will. You can instruct them on how to open the damn thing without destroying everything." She glares at me and crawls over Knox and out of the bed. "You cannot and you will not. I need to go. I have to be there. And, for that matter, some lady popped into my dream," she pauses as she puts her arms into the robe and cinches it up at her waist, "just to make sure I knew about this. I think it might be important that I be the one to go. If you are so worried about the danger, then you better send plenty of guards."

I stand and yell at her, "I said you will not be going, and that's final!"

She puts her hands on her hips and smiles sweetly, "Sunshine, you can either take me there well guarded or I will bloody well go there myself. You won't find them without me."

Knox starts laughing and we both turn to look at him. "You may as well let her go well guarded. We can go with her. No one could protect her better. We'll take plenty of guards and be done with it. Besides, if She is in on this, you aren't going to win and you know it. Yelling won't change that. But maybe you should try having a full on tantrum?"

My shoulders drop. "I just want her safe. That's all."

Valdís crosses the room to lay a hand on my heart and her head on my arm, "I'll try really hard to stay alive for you, ok?"

I wrap my arms around her in a bear hug. "I guess that will have to do."

Fifteen

They are so cute over there hugging it out as he bends to her will. Why he thought that he would get his way on that, I can't imagine. Personally, the fact that she was so reasonable about guards made me fully willing to go along with it. That and the fact that the goddess that made us what we are now is poking her lovely nose into Valdís' dreams about it. Her bringing it to Valdís's attention was nothing more than her way of telling us without talking to us that this is how it will be.

A knock sounds and Valdís looks at me as Malic shows no signs of being ready to release her. I nod with a grin and get up to answer the door. Epaphras is on the other side and as Valdís is fully robed, I just let him in, not like he hasn't seen us with our dicks out a million or so times over the years.

He steps in and quietly says, "Sire, we have a bit of a problem."

I look at Malic, who has one eye open and focused over here now. He nods and I turn back to Epaphras, "Go ahead with it."

Epaphras' eyes widen, but he recovers fast. "It would appear that a large, rather thorny hedge has sprung up around the palace. Around all the palaces."

"I see. Are the tunnels affected?"

He shakes his head. "Not currently, no."

"Ok, meet us in the office. We'll be there as soon as we can shower and get dressed." He nods and lets himself out, closing the door softly behind himself. I turn back to them. "Looks like your field trip will be delayed, Valdís. We need to shower and get out there. This is likely to be a long day." Malic meets my eyes as he releases Valdís and I nod, knowing he feels the same as I do. She is staying with one or both of us outside this room from now on.

* * *

Malic

It takes some time to get Valdís tucked away in the office with Knox and a book, but once she is, I come out to the rampart with Epaphras to survey the extent of the plant growth. Epaphras insisted I see it from up here before I walk the grounds outside the castle. He is going on about the plant being some sort of hybrid as we make it to the rampart and I look out over the land before me. Epaphras tells me that one part of the hybrid is a plant called crown of thorns and it is quite toxic.

But that isn't what frightens me as I look out at the massive wall of it. No, what frightens me is that it is still growing inward. Not fast enough that Epaphras could see it from here, but I can. This plant is on the attack and I don't know how to stop it. We have to get Valdís somewhere safe. I can't lose her. Pulling the satellite phone from the inner pocket of my jacket, I send a message to my brothers, "Come home. Now." Expecting no answer, I put it away. I know they will get here as quickly as possible and they will get in touch with Epaphras even faster. Looking over at him, I say, "Be expecting them."

He blanches, recovering he says, "All of you will be home? At the same time?"

"As soon as they can get here." I wave a hand at the plant wall, "That plant is still growing, and it is growing toward the castle at a rate that isn't possible. This is magic. The outsiders are here and we are under attack."

Epaphras runs for the stairs and I turn to stare out at the ever-growing wall of thorns.

Sixteen

Eirene

I hate having that fool Ingemar over, for any reason. Even this report. I am already well aware of how the rally went, but I need to compare what I know with what that fool tells me, or doesn't. Somehow I think he is going to neglect to mention the meeting afterward at his home. I will have to jog his memory.

Flavi knocks on my office door and pokes her head in. "He is here. Should I show him in now or make him wait?"

Seating myself at the desk, I tell her, "Walk slowly back and show him in, don't rush."

A few long minutes later, Ingemar is shown in, red in the face at the slowness of my Flavi. "Your help walks as though she is lamed Eirene. You should see to that."

I raise a brow at him and gesture for him to sit while I finish signing some paperwork. I can hear his teeth grinding at the wait. Good. An angry man is an incautious one. When I set my pen down and look up, I am almost certain another five minutes would have given him a heart attack. Something to remember for when his usefulness has run out.

"Tell me, Ingemar, how have my plans gone thus far?"

He rolls his shoulders before answering. "It went very well. You know, I am sure, of the case being dismissed and the papers picking it up. I assume you saw the stories. Lord Judda arranged a rally, Pelos and myself spoke at it. The crowds were very supportive. I think our plan to discredit the kings is working very well."

Picking up my pen, I start making varied strokes on the paper before me. When I look up again, I ask, "And is that all that has happened?"

He looks distinctly uncomfortable as he says, "What do you mean?"

"Care to tell me why Lord Judda and some others showed up at your home not long after the rally?"

Tugging his sleeves, he says, "Oh that! Well, those lords have an idea about staging a coup on the kings. They've made a loose plan to gather some assassins and send them in to murder the current king in place. Then they are to pick off the incoming kings as they awaken. It really isn't a bad plan."

Nodding, I say, "I see. Well, I will ensure that the wall

of thorns has a hole for those assassins to enter the palace grounds through."

He looks at me, eyes wide and mouth open, "Wall of thorns? Whatever are you talking about?"

Laughing at his surprise, I tell him, "My God gave me a plant. He said when the time was right, I would take the plant to the castle and plant it in a very particular place. Once planted, it would grow and spread. Effectively trapping the king in the castle. That original plant is the key to the whole thing, but no one will be able to find it. So now, there is a massive wall of poisonous thorny vines surrounding each of the castles."

He laughs. "It certainly sounds effective. But how do you know the kings won't just cut their way out?"

Just then, Flavi knocks on the door and pops her head in. "Mistress, you said you wanted the papers immediately?"

"I do Flavi, bring them in now." She crosses the room at her usual quick pace. Ingemar scowls at seeing it and narrows his eyes at me. I shrug as Flavi lays the papers on my desk. She bows and leaves the room just as quickly. The paper on top has a beautiful picture of my thorny wall. I smile and pass that one to Ingemar. "Here, have a look for yourself."

I pick up the next in the stack to peruse after he takes the first from my hand. He reads fast and looks up. "Holy shit. And you say these are around each castle?"

"They are. No one will enter or leave without my say."

And you should be grateful that my god says you are still needed.

Ingemar

Lord Judda and the others are waiting for me when I arrive home. That bitch Eirene could fuck up all our plans! Making a split second decision, I decide to trust the other lords with the information about Eirene and her part in this.

Once I have spent my ire telling them about her latest trick, they are quiet for a bit. Lord Judda eventually says, "This could work. What she has done is not without benefit. She is useful right now. At some point when her usefulness is gone, she will simply have a little accident."

I look up from my drink, "What about her god? Won't that be a problem?"

Lord Judda gets a sly look on his face. "What is a deity without their follower? Everyone else here either follows our goddess or no one. When she dies, so will his power on our continent. Simple math. If the daughter with her follows him, she'll have to have her own accident."

Smiling, I tell him, "Judda, I never knew you were so devious."

He scoffs, "It isn't the sort of thing one wants to be

known for in all circles. You know, since she isn't from here, we could easily poison her with something native that won't hurt us. One little drink and suddenly, she is gone and her problems with her. Besides, Conrí should never have married the little tart, anyway. We all tried to tell him she was just an outsider and wanted him only for his status. He didn't want to believe us. Wouldn't, until about a year ago. Then he wanted to know how I knew she was an outsider."

An outsider? Well, that's interesting. "How did you know? Is there a way to recognize them?"

Judda looks surprised at first. "Oh yes, I forget how young you are, Ingemar. You weren't around when the uprising happened. It's so easy to forget these things. The outsiders had staged a murder of our kings a long time ago. They killed over half of them in a surprise attack. When the surviving kings recovered, they banished all the outsiders. Some of them were so smug. How would anyone prove their lineage? The kings were all set to tell them about the records when everyone that was an outsider suddenly grabbed their ear and started screaming. HER voice rang out through the land. She said something like this is my land and all those not my people will bear this mark so long as they are on my land. Sure enough, when they stopped screaming, you could see a small, red cross in the hollow behind their earlobe. You can bet that Eirene still has hers. Our goddess has a long memory and a vicious temper."

"Well, that is enlightening. And it doesn't matter if they are born here?"

"No. The outsiders are different and the few still here continue to be born with the mark."

Seventeen

VALDÍS

The scream rips from my throat as I reach out to hold the door. Anything to stop them from getting in. But the door disappears under my fingers and I open my eyes to see a king on either side of me in the dark, each hugging me and trying to calm me. My heart is still racing as I tell them, "They're coming!"

Knox asks, "Who is coming?" while Malic rubs my back.

I scramble off the bed. "No! You don't understand! THEY ARE COMING! They have their own passage and they are coming to kill you!"

Knox hits the lamp, and the light brings the room into focus for me. Malic is already putting his pants on. As the door opens to one of my guards poking his head in, Malic tells them, "Come in and close the door behind you."

They believe me and that lets my heart slow its frantic pace a little. Knox motions the guards over as he slips on his pants. I hear him telling them, "The castle is infiltrated. You are going with Valdís. Protect her at all costs, understand? If we die, get her to the other kings. Do not let her die under any circumstances."

Even as my jaw drops, a fully clothed Malic grabs my arm and drags me over to the closet. Shoving my clothing aside, he searches the back wall with his fingertips while telling me, "We need you to hide in here. Whatever may come for us, please stay in here. With you safe, we can do the terrible things we are about to do. I will do everything in my power to come back to get you, but I can't focus on that if I am terrified that they will get to you." His finger hits a tiny button and the back of the closet swings into a dark hall behind it. He turns to really look at me for the first time since he started talking, and I can see the fear in his eyes. My mind flashes back to the garden and as much as I would like to fight this, I can't. I can't put him through that agony. So when he says, "Will you do this for me?"

I can answer no other way than to nod. "Yes. I will. I don't like it, but I will."

He nods and kisses me softly. "We will come back for you if I have to bathe this kingdom in blood to do it." Pulling back, he helps me over the ledge into the dark hall. The guards follow, with hand held lamps they start down the hall while I linger to watch the door shut.

Malic

I could hear the way Valdís's heart was racing before she woke up in a scream. Mine has matched pace with hers since I realized that my worst fears were coming to fresh life tonight. Turning away from the secret passage I just sent Valdís down, I immediately turn back and slide her clothing back into place. The gown she was wearing is thin, but there should be blankets. The guards will care for her. I sent Epaphras the message that we are under attack while I was getting dressed.

I look over at Knox as I turn to face the room. "You know, you could go with her. Help keep her safe. Keep yourself safe. Protect the continent by staying alive."

Knox turns off the light, walks over and puts his hands on my shoulders, looking into my eyes as he says, "This isn't like when we lost them. They think it is only me here. We haven't announced your presence. They may want to kill me and Valdís, but they have no idea you have come home. Thanks to Valdís, and very probably our goddess, we have the element of surprise on our side. It will be different this time."

I nod and take a deep breath. "Let's go then."

Knox releases my shoulders, and we head for the door.

Knox

With Malic at my back, I open the door the slightest crack and slowly open it further, as I don't see or hear anyone. I make sure to look up because my time spent with the outsiders has not been wasted and I know very well that people hide up there. However, there is no one in this hallway and we ease the door fully open before having a more thorough look both ways. Malic motions for me to take the wall on the far side of the hall and once I am there, we both creep toward the end of the hall. We get there and freeze, seeing a group of people creeping along the hallway intersecting our hall, until we realize those are our men. Malic steps into their field of vision. They stop as a group to inspect before creeping over to enter our hall. Leaving two men to keep watch, we take the rest into the first room. It hasn't been used in a long time but, he would be happy to play a part in routing these fuckers. They tell us they heard noises outside, that sounded like fighting, but Epaphras let everyone know about the attack before they heard those noises, so possibly it went well.

Malic takes the lead, telling them that half the group will go with me to search the upstairs. The other half is with him downstairs. I realize he is keeping me upstairs because he is hoping they will all be downstairs, but no one outside the castle is aware that Valdís's room has been changed. I feel pretty certain there will be someone in her old room or on the way to it. Malic is done giving his directions and we leave the room, splitting our groups at the end of the hallway. Malic flips me off before he turns to go, his way of saying he will come find me if I die.

We are cursory with the search for most of the upstairs, but then we get to the wing where Valdís was staying. The first guy never sees us as one of the guards slips up behind him and, with a sharp twist to the right, snaps his neck and lays him gently on the floor. Two of them push his body so he is laying across the middle of the hall. A fine trip hazard for anyone that tries to run away. Two more doorways down the hall, the door to Valdís's old room is open and someone in there sounds angry. We decide to keep these for later questioning. We get set outside the room while they are still making enough noise, cursing about where to find her that we could have an entire patrol out here marching and still not be heard. After managing to get all of us into the room behind them, I have two guards sneak up behind them and just give their heads a little tap. Just enough to knock them out. Only one saw it coming, and that was because Jackson swung faster than Robert. I chose not to hit them because I might accidentally rip off a body part and beat them with it before I realized what I was doing and I don't think I could pull the punch enough to keep them alive if I did stay in control.

As it turns out, the things they were saying they were going to do when they found her were real damn offensive and I don't want to fuck up the opportunity to work on them in a more... methodical manner. My guards tie them up well, tying hands and feet very well before tying them up face to face. Hopefully, they don't struggle too much before they figure out about the rope around their necks.

Leaving Valdís's old room we continue on, finding another set with some of our employees and Dagma cornered in a room, They are trying to force them to reveal where to find anyone else in the castle, but mostly where to find my Valdís, there are three of them. My people are refusing, one of the men just told them in a most creative manner exactly how to go about fucking themselves right out of the castle before the king finds them. They are all getting raises just for that. I run into the room and grab the leader, his hands on the throat of my guy with the smart mouth, and I snatch his head round up and off his shoulders. The strength she gave us does in fact, do something more than reassure Valdís that I won't be hurt if she leaps that fine ass onto me. Knox, you are covered in the blood of your enemy. Maybe not the best time for these thoughts?

None of my people seem upset by the head removal and Dagma looks rather surprisingly pleased. The other two men have been collected by my guards. Another of my guards produces rope and I ask, "Do you always carry rope around on your person?"

One of them laughs, "No. Epaphras has stashes of various items secreted all over the castle. We have been raiding those since we started collecting people. I would offer you a weapon, but it seems kind of pointless considering."

"Yes, indeed." We leave two of my guards with them to watch over the ones we tied up and guard our people against any further abuse. After I drag the other two into the room with the others. Wouldn't want them to feel left out. We trace our steps back the way we came after I barricade the door to the back stairs. If there is only one way up, that makes our job a little easier.

We find one more guy starting down into the king's wing and knock him out too. Myself and two guards stand watch while the third guard drops him off in the room with everyone else.

When he returns, we head for the stairs.

Eighteen

Malic

At the bottom of the stairs, I stop and scent the air. I follow the scent of someone to the kitchen. Slipping in, I see a man in the pantry opening the food stores and mixing them before closing them very neatly and moving on to the next. I can't imagine what... poison. They are trying to poison her. Us. Valdís. She would have no chance if—a fiery rage courses through my body and when I come to again, the man is dead. His body is in pieces, everywhere.

I realize they just watched me tear a man into much smaller pieces than he started in and I say, "I'm sorry. I didn't mean to lose control like that. I realized he was poisoning our food and..."

I hang my head in shame, but one of them speaks up,

"Sire, our families eat that food, too. We aren't bothered by what you did. Any one of us would have done the same had we the strength you have. So don't worry about it."

I take a deep breath, "Ok then. I need one of you to stay here and ensure that no one eats anything from these stores."

The one that reassured me volunteers and I thank him, clapping a hand on his shoulder as we pass. The rest of the men follow me out and down the hall. I head for the king's office, our communal office that is more well known about. Spotting two men in there going through documents and stealing whatever they deem important, I decide we will knock them out for future questioning because they obviously had a much different assignment than what the others had.

I use my speed to get in the room and hit each once before they even realize they aren't alone. Funny how I can do that with men trying to steal royal secrets as opposed to the ones speaking such foul words about my mate. We search them and find a lot of papers tucked away on their bodies. After my men tied them up, we decide to hang them upside down from the ceiling until one of us has time to collect them. Happily, we used this room for other purposes a long time ago. It has good, sturdy o rings mounted up there. While they take care of hanging the two spies from the ceiling, I spot our old swords on the wall.

It is a large display, all twelve swords, one for each of

us, that started out saving our homeland. I touch one with a very plain hilt, remembering Leopold and how he made this plain sword look magical as he danced with it. Killing made beautiful. My men have finished and are waiting quietly for me. I tip my head at the swords of the men who were like my brothers and I take mine down.

The blade is still as sharp as the day I last used it. I turn to leave and think better of it, turning back to grab Knox's sword as well. He might need it. We stop in the doorway, watching as some of our guards slip through the main area, skirting the open spaces. I start for the next hall, the men behind me.

A knife flashes and my chest burns as I come even with a vase. I lean back and swing my sword. I feel the blood splash before I hear the screams begin. The knife and the forearm of my attacker lay on the floor. My men bandage him to slow the bleeding as I pick up the knife. Sniffing it, I can smell my blood and the sap of the plant outside. "They've poisoned their blades. Pass on the warning." The burning is annoying but begins to fade quickly, as it was just a shallow cut. My men have the man that cut me quiet now. I should have paid better attention. He should never have gotten that close without my knowing. Dammit! This kind of idiocy is what gets people killed. We start to walk away from the bloody mess and realize that we are tracking the blood as we go. "Take off your shoes and we will finish our check."

As we do that, Knox comes toward us, calling out in a whisper when he sees me. I motion him to come forward and I hand him his sword. He tells me, "Pretty sure between you and me we have found them all. The guards out front died from sheer numbers. The guards in the garage, we helped even the score for them and they are cleaning that up now. That reminds me, what did the guy all over the kitchen do to be spread about like that?"

My eyes narrow and my jaw clenches. "He poisoned our food. He was poisoning it all when I walked in. They meant to kill Valdís, whether or not they managed the coup. And they didn't care how many they killed with her." I run a hand across the back of my neck. "I may have lost control when I realized that and only came to after he was in pieces."

Knox frowns and nods. Then he shrugs. "That was probably the kinder thing to do. A lot nicer than the tortures I would have inflicted on his person for trying to kill our Valdís. We caught a couple that planned some really atrocious things for her, they are currently tied up. Oh, we caught quite a few hiding in the gardens. They didn't seem to be expecting us to search there. I suppose they thought they were safe."

Epaphras comes out of a side hall with his own set of guards and a blood-stained sword. He appears physically fine. All the blood on him doesn't smell like his, so I tell him, "The food in the kitchen has been poisoned. I want you to check in with the other castles, see if there were matching attacks, or did they focus on this castle because they knew Knox was here. If all is well, send some guards through the tunnels to get food from the other castles."

He dips his head, "Yes, sir. May I just say it really is nice to see two of you here at the same time? Maybe having all of you here again will be a good thing."

Knox barks a laugh. "A better thing if we hadn't just been attacked by our own people."

Nineteen

VALDÍS

We have been in this room for the better part of eternity at this point. It is chilly and damp feeling down here; the guards wrapped me in blankets as soon as we finished descending all those bloody stairs.

They don't want to talk and so I just sit here, seeing bits and pieces of my dream over and over again. The men pouring through the hole in the thorny wall.

Knox dying at the hands of some guy all in black when he runs into his office. Malic meeting his end in my old bedroom. Dead guards everywhere. Her voice as she shouted, "Sound the alarm or all will be lost! Wake up and sound the alarm!"

Her voice was everywhere, through and over the visions in my dream. Even the screams of the dying held the echoes of her warning. The guards are suddenly excited. They move away from the stairwell they have been guarding this entire time. Then I hear them. Oh thank the Goddess, they are safe!

They round the last corner and come into my sight. I fly out of the blankets, running and leaping at them. They catch me like I weigh nothing. They attempt to hug me but they are covered in blood and I am checking to ensure that none of it is theirs. I find the hole in Malic's shirt where he was sliced. The wound seems healed, if a little angry. Knox picks me up and carries me up the stairs, holding me close the entire way.

As if they had agreed before they got to me. When we get back to my room, Malic sits down in the big chair I favor and Knox sets me on his lap. I'm not upset about this at all. Knox sits down in the chair across from this one and asks, "How did you know?"

I look him in the eyes and tell him, "You know how I knew. I had a dream. She showed me what they would do if I didn't wake up. What they would do to you, how you would both die." My voice catches as I try not to outright sob. "It was horrible. And through all that she showed me, I could hear her screaming at me to sound the alarm."

Malic says, "She who?"

My brows drop and my eyes narrow. "She who? The same she that told me you were watching me sleep like a creeper."

Malic and Knox share a look and Knox says, "Could you describe her?"

Nodding, I tell them, "Her hair is dark, like those nights where there is no moon, no stars, just night so dark you can't see your hand in front of your face. Her skin is a darker olive tone, like mine. Her eyes are gray like storm clouds. It is always dark in the dreams when she comes to me, never more light than the moon, stars, and the dark glow from her. For all the low light, I never have a problem seeing her. When I ask her about it, she just laughs."

Malic nods and looks over at Knox. "It's her. You know as well as I that it is her in Valdís's dreams."

Knox chuckles, "Still harboring any doubts she is the queen, oh brother in arms?"

Malic shakes his head no. "I don't. She can't be anyone else. But everyone has to agree. It can't be declared officially until the rest of us have agreed."

Knox asks, "When will they be here?"

Malic shrugs, "Soon. I sent a message. Epaphras probably has a better timetable."

I have been silent this entire time as I let them reveal things while they mostly forgot I was here, but now I need to know, "Do you really know who she is? The lady in my dreams? What do all the kings need to agree on? Why does it seem like you mean me when you talk about someone being queen? Why are all the kings coming here?"

Knox sighs, "We do. It is our Goddess. The Goddess

of our land. She of the keys and torches to light the way. She caused everyone to forget her name when the others attacked the first time. She is the one that gave us the blessing story. And the other one, about when we would be blessed with the one we had waited for, the one we never imagined would take so long to arrive."

I don't know at all what to think about this. Why would she be in my dreams instead of talking to them? Blessed with who? "Why isn't she talking to you all?"

Malic chuckles. "She might be somewhat annoyed with us."

"Why? What did you do?"

Knox rubs his chin. "We might have gone through a century or so of drunken debauchery because we didn't have faith that our Goddess's plan was still in motion. It would seem she is still holding a grudge."

"Oh. Is she mad about the lack of faith or the drunken debauchery?"

Malic laughs, "Definitely the lack of faith. She has no issues with drunken debauchery as long as it doesn't interfere with the work to be done."

"Ah, I see. I can't blame her. She specifically told you something, and you decided not to believe her. Kind of like calling her a liar. Who were you supposed to be blessed with?"

Knox looks directly at me. "You."

"Um, what?"

"She promised us that there would be a queen. A woman to match us all, that would live as long as us, that would be one of us. She was really specific that she was not a reward, but that she would eventually be a part of the defense of this land."

"What? That can't be me. I can't even take care of myself or my people. How the hell would I be able to help defend the entire place?"

Malic sighs. "You have much more potential than you believe, and there is always the possibility of things locked inside."

I shake my head, "No. There is nothing special in me. Of that I am sure. Why did she make everyone forget her name?"

"Because she didn't want people to remember exactly who she is. Or what she can do. She said it would be important one day," Knox laughs. "She didn't tell us when that day would be, either."

"Ok, why are the kings on their way here now?"

"Because we are under siege. Someone meant to keep us locked away in the castle till they could come kill us. Which they attempted tonight. And we aren't the only ones they had plans for. There were people sent looking for you as well."

Looking down at the floor, I tell them, "I know."

Malic's arms tighten around me. "She showed you, didn't she?"

I nod, not having words for what those people want to do to me.

Knox says, "We aren't letting that happen. No matter what."

Malic says, "Perhaps it wouldn't be a bad thing for you to learn how to defend yourself."

Knox

A knock sounds on the door and since Malic is still talking Valdís into learning how to defend herself, I get up to answer it. Epaphras is at the door. I let him in and we stand just a little away from the door as he tells me, "Sire, the men we captured. I have bad news about a large number of them."

"Oh no, what now? Did they escape?"

"In a manner of speaking, yes. They died. The ones the castle employees were helping to monitor. They are all still alive. One of the ones that was in the office is still with us because a guard saw what was going on and threw a knife at him. Pretty much all the rest are dead."

Rubbing the back of my neck with one hand, I feel something sloughing off and I bring my hand in front of me to look. Fuck, we are still covered in blood. "I need a shower. Ok, what have you done with the ones that are still alive?"

"Well, sire, I had them stripped of all their clothing and thoroughly searched. Then I put them in cells naked with no sheets or blankets. I did turn up the temperature down there. I feel I should mention that Dagma knocked out the ones that were being watched over by the castle employees. When I asked her why, she said, and I quote, 'It's real fucking hard to poison yourself if you are unconscious.'"

I grin. I like that Dagma more and more. "Well, she is not wrong. It's a shame though. I had hoped to question all of them."

"I do have some other news, though I can't say it is really any better."

"Fucking hell. All right, let's hear it."

Epaphras swallows and I know it must be bad, "Some of our people, the ones we had watching them? They came in after the group that attacked us. They weren't in time to save the guards out front, but they came in and helped the other guards with finding the rest. I have been able to collect their reports, and it isn't good. Not good at all."

"I am glad they are back, safe and with news. Now please, get to the news. Blood itches when it dries on the skin."

"Oh! Yes, sire. It would seem that this was meant to be a coup. There is a group of Lords waiting for word that this attack was successful, so they can wander in and take the castle over, along with Ms. Valdís."

The growl rips from my throat at the mention of them taking her. "My apologies Epaphras. I know roughly what they had planned for her, so that idea is upsetting."

He nods, "Yes. One of them is still quite upset about it.

How did he phrase that? Oh yes, being denied that pussy, they promised him."

Malic chooses that moment to suddenly deposit a very confused Valdís in my arms as he says, "We'll tend to that later, Knox. Epaphras, make sure not another one of them dies. If there is even a slight possibility of an explosion killing them, move them underground. Station guards watching the new entrance and keep them away from the vines. Make certain they understand that those thorns are likely to kill them. I will come find you shortly and we will discuss further security measures."

Epaphras nods, "As you wish, sire."

Malic

Epaphras turns to go and then back, "Sire, I think you should perhaps know the rest. Sooner rather than later. Perhaps you could step outside with me so we could discuss it without Valdís having to hear it?"

Valdís pulls a rather impressive move where she manages to swing her legs up and spin herself at the same time, landing mostly on her feet with Knox gripping her arms to keep her upright now that she has jumped out of his hold. I don't think she planned that move as it takes her a moment to gather herself before she turns to face Epaphras, "You may as well say it in front of me now. I will find out. Or, if you like, I could go snooping through the entire castle until I find out what it is. Of course, who knows what else I will find along the way…"

Shaking my head, I grit out, "Just go ahead and say it. Save us the trouble of repeating it."

Epaphras draws a breath. "As you wish. Our people also reported that at a meeting in the house of Ingemar, a decision was made about Valdís. The decision is why the men were after her tonight." He looks away. "They decided that since she has been whoring herself for the king anyway, they are going to use that to their advantage. The plan is to get her pregnant, and whether or not she is right now, they will claim it belongs to Knox. At the same time, her mind is to be broken completely so that she cannot argue with them. The blame for that will be placed on Knox as well. The men that were searching for her in her old room were to start the process." He looks back at me with his face composed once again. "He is the one that continued to shout about getting Valdís. He shouted until one of the guards could take it no more. He only hit him the one time and we are fairly certain he will wake up."

The rage that I felt before I heard this was nothing. An annoyance compared to this. With a growl, I grab the sword I had left leaned against the wall when I entered the room, fully intending to go and make one hell of a mess. Before I can take a step, Valdís jumps in front of me, all fire and fear. "No! No, you can't! This is what they want!" Her hands are flat on my chest like she would hold me in place. I hold still to keep from hurting her and let her speak. "Malic, these lords that are running this show, them and my stepmother, they want you to be outraged and tear them into little bits. Those people are doing exactly what they have been taught and told to do. If you murder them like this, they will use it to turn the rest of the people against you. Please," she lays her head on my chest and inhales, "please do not play into their hands. When you play chess, you don't spend all your time taking out the pawns. I assure you, my stepmother has played many games and she will sacrifice pawns all day long to meet her goal."

Knox shrugs. "She would know her better than we do."

Valdís looks up at me. "This is what they do. They pull dirty, underhanded things like this. Things no one will see. Then, when the outcome is discovered, they will paint you all as the bad guys. Wanton murderers with no conscience whatsoever. Not fit to rule. Monsters. You know many of the things that my stepmother did to me. She always had an alibi, an excuse, a reason why someone else was the guilty one. Her stories were so convincing that I wondered sometimes if I had seen things correctly. That is what they will do to you. She is not the only one that plays the world that way. It was one of the things my father hated the most about the lords here. You have to be smarter than them. More controlled than them."

My head knows she is right. My heart is screaming that I have to kill them, kill them, kill them, keep them away from her at all costs. I look into her eyes and I can't do it. I can't cause her that hurt and worry when she is technically safe from them right now. I set my sword back against the wall. "All right. I won't kill them this time. Come on, let's get a shower. All this will be a lot easier to tolerate if I am not constantly hungered by all the blood on us."

Twenty

Eirene

Maxwell has made it back safely from his assignment and I am eager to hear what he has to report. Even if the hour is quite late and I was woken from a delicious sleep by my Flavi. With my robe securely in place, I leave my quarters and walk toward my office.

I find Maxwell has helped himself to a drink but is still standing and bows when I enter. He looks rather beaten as well, so I will give him a pass this time.

Moving to seat myself behind my desk, I gesture for him to sit as well. He nearly collapses into the chair and I wonder what exactly happened. I suppose he will tell me all about it. I hope he keeps the story short. I really need my beauty sleep. "Ok Maxwell, tell me, how did their coup go?"

He takes another gulp from his glass, swallows it down and says, "In a word, poorly. They were well prepared for attack and the castle is like a maze. The guards they hired are worth every penny. The men out front were killed, and it seemed like all would go well. They split into factions and started searching the entire place. A few went to the garage to clear the men there. I followed, staying well out of sight. They were expecting them. And there are two kings in place right now."

I can't have heard that right. "What did you say?"

He holds up two fingers. "Two! I said there are two kings in place right now. King Knox is there and awake, but King Malic is also awake. There haven't been any announcements! None of the men were expecting it. But the kings and the guards knew before they should have that they were under attack. They must have an informant. That's the only way they could have known."

Shit! Two! This is not good. And the coup failed. I have to call him to me. HE won't be happy. But surely he won't blame me. How was I to know? And dealing with these idiot lords...

"But that isn't all. That isn't the worst of it."

My eyes narrow at him. "What do you mean, that isn't the worst of it?"

"They have other plans kept secret from you. Plans that are distasteful, no matter how you feel about Valdís."

"Tell me. What plans have these lords made that are so foul, it bothers even you?" He tells me of the one that was assigned to begin the breaking of Valdís, how he looked forward to making sure she would be pregnant if the kings hadn't already gotten her with child. How he discussed his plans to begin breaking her in great detail to anyone that would listen or even pretend to. He is correct, the plans these idiot lords made are disgusting. Vile in ways that bother even me, as much as I want her dead.

Then he goes on, "That lady you had the other men after? She was spotted entering the castle."

I feel the blood draining from my face. Dagma could ruin everything! She can't be allowed to live!

I sit up straighter in my chair. "Priorities are changed. Dagma must die. Preferably Valdís dies too, but above all, Dagma must die. I don't care if you have to stand in trees and shoot her through a fucking window. She must die now. Then, Valdís. Make sure she is killed now. I want news of Dagma's death by the afternoon. Go, clean up and get out there. Are the men that were supposed to bring her in still following her? Are they watching her from outside the castle?"

His head bobs once. "They are. It was them that asked me to pass the news on."

"Good. Tell them orders are changed. Kill her now. I don't care who else has to die so long as they kill her immediately."

He leaves the room and I pour myself a drink from the secret stash. These HE brought me from the world my people came from. The world I desperately want to be a part of but can't because my ancestors chose wrong. If I can't go there, I will fucking rule here and open the place back up. It is long past time that our little continent opened to the outsiders again. Maybe once it is opened and their goddess gone, this fucking cross behind my ear will go away. The kings should have laid down and died to become myths a long time ago. But no. They just sit up in that stupid castle, waiting for some attack that will never come because the real outsiders don't care about us. They have their own problems. Thankfully, the god I share with them does care.

How the fuck did Dagma make it there? What has she told the kings? It will be fine. Surely she didn't just run up there and immediately spill her guts about Valdís. She isn't that smart. Protection! Yes! That's it! She went there since Valdís is there because she needed protection. That must be it! Still, the sooner she dies, the better. Some secrets must be buried.

Ingemar

A single bedraggled and bloody man is the one that comes to report to us. Seeing him, all I can think about is that nothing went right. He performs the usual social niceties and I give him leave to report. Every one of the lords is watching Judda especially closely.

"Sir, we were routed. It was an ambush. I don't know

how they knew, but they knew. And there are two kings in the castle right now."

Two? My intel said that only one was awake right now! I press my lips together briefly. "Tell me all that happened. I want the full report."

"We got in just fine. We handled the guards out front real nice and quiet. Then we split into groups and went inside. That's when it all went wrong. They waited until we were fully split up into weaker factions spread throughout the castle. Then guards and kings were suddenly everywhere. Our men are mostly dead. The ones that weren't killed outright were taken prisoner. The ones taken prisoner all tried to kill themselves, but only one succeeded before I made it out of there. The rest were stripped and searched very thoroughly. I believe they are in the prison now though I cannot verify that."

Lord Judda is suddenly very pale as he says, "We cannot allow them to be questioned. This is why we sent men willing to die if they were captured. Those kings have to die. We cannot allow this to be connected to us unless they are dead. We could lose everything!"

"Let me think for a minute. We can turn this in our favor, somehow. I just need some quiet. Give me five minutes of peace!" Pacing the space behind my desk, I try to sort through the information we have. No one knows we sent men up there. No one but the men that we pay. No one knows... I stop as an idea strikes. "I have it. I know how we can make it seem like the kings attacked us for going to speak with them, how we can paint them to be savages that can't control their blood thirst. But we are going to need some bruises first."

Lord Judda smiles. "Just what do you have in mind?"

Twenty-One

Valdís

The kings both seem to think that the goddess is talking to me in my dreams, but somehow I think they are either crazy or just trying to humor me. Why would she talk to me? I am nobody. Surely not even a worthy messenger. I am left to my own devices right now. The kings both think I am in my room, but I couldn't stand being cooped up in there anymore. Two of the guards are following me, sticking close, their eyes never stopping their slow scan of the area.

I hate it that the castle was breached. That all this started because I couldn't just accept my fate. I couldn't leave well enough alone. My people would have survived, I am sure. They just wouldn't be as well off as they were under my father's rule. And it is possible that Eumeleia would be a good ruler for them. I should have just let Eirene kill me one of the many times she tried.

Stumbling over a rug, I take notice of my surroundings and realize that I am in front of the library. I haven't had anything to read in forever, it seems. Pushing the doors open, I enter and just stare. This room is enormous. My guards brush past me and check the entire room. I wait by the entrance. I know they are really serious about this and so are the kings. I don't want them to get in trouble because I didn't let them do their jobs. They come back to the entrance and one tells me, "We will guard the entrance if you would like to wander the stacks for a time. We can give you that much privacy."

"Thank you. You are the best, and I appreciate you giving me what space you can. I think I will wander in here for a time."

He nods and they station themselves outside the library with the doors still open. I wander through the shelves. The books are amazing. Strange. Many of them appear to be by people I don't think are from here. Hmm, this might be the place to learn more about our Goddess and what she looks like. What she could possibly want with me, of all people.

But where would I start looking? I've barely had the idea, and it is already hopeless. What if, maybe? I vaguely remember an old story about a woman that could find things if she focused on them. I look around to make sure no one is in here to see me try something so very foolish. It seems clear, I can't even see the guards from here.

Closing my eyes, I focus on the image of the lady in my dream, the sound of her voice, the smell of cool clear night time air that seems to hover around her. I feel a strange pull building inside me and I open my eyes to follow the pull as it leads me down one aisle, through a break and into another. I follow it deep into the library, finding a section that is darker, cooler. Like the heat and light aren't penetrating this area as well. Slowing, I realize that I was near running to follow the pull into this section of the library. My hand lifts to trail along a shelf, oddly collecting no dust along the way. I see it. The book that I am looking for. The cover is made of some sort of cloth, deep blue. There is no title on the spine, but I know this is the book I need.

I reach out to pull it down, but pause. Should I pull this book out? I've caused so much trouble following my heart already. Do I want to risk it? Can I go back to the world if I don't? I don't think I can leave here without seeing what is in this book. Finding out if it holds the answers to the questions I have. I reach up and snatch the book off the shelf and hold it close to me before I can change my mind.

My heart is racing as I look for a place to sit and open the tome. Moving through the room, I find a chair with a small table next to it. Looking around to make sure no one can see me, I sit down. Laying the book on the table, I lift the table and set it directly in front of me. There are no words on the front of the book either. My hand hovers over the book, heart racing as I stare down at it. Dare I?

I've come this far, but I haven't opened it. I could turn back. I could push the book into a random shelf and run away. No one would be the wiser.

Except me. I would know that I was too scared to open the book that could maybe answer my questions. Maybe it could give me answers to questions I didn't know I had. One deep breath in and I put my hand on the cover and open it before I can have any more doubts.

Inside the front cover, on the first page, is her. The exact image of the woman in my dreams. Her smile seems almost to be daring me to seek more inside the book. To turn the page with her image and see what lies within. How could I not?

Hand shaking, I do it. I turn the page and find her name. Our Goddess has a name? Why would it be hidden in this book? Why wouldn't we have been calling her by name all this time? I turn the page and find what looks to be the history of her. Picking the book up and leaning back in the chair, I settle in to read it.

* * *

I am reading the last page when one of the guards taps me on the shoulder and scares the life out of me. A scream rips from my throat, and I am left gasping, the book clutched to my chest, "Fucking hells! Make some damn noise when you walk! How does a man your size not make more noise? Goddess above, what do you want?"

The other guard stopped running to help well out of reach and seems to be struggling not to laugh, the bastard. The one in front of me is blushing like mad as he says, "My apologies. But you didn't seem to hear me when I said your name. I would not have touched you otherwise."

And now my cheeks are heating. "Damn. I'm sorry, I was deep in this book. I hope you will forgive my abrupt manner."

His face twists like he is trying not to laugh, and he says, "I wanted to tell you that it is nearing time for dinner. If you don't want the kings to know you left your room without them, you should head back now. Before Epaphras comes to find you."

"Oh, yes. Do you think anyone will mind if I take this book to my room? I wish to reread some portions of it."

He looks down at the book still clutched to my chest and back to my eyes. "No, I think no one will mind. Especially not for you."

"Good!" I close the book and tuck it under my arm, leading the way out of the library and back to my room. Once I get in there and they have thoroughly checked it and made their exit to stand outside, I open the book and finish the last page. It's a ritual. Meant for witches. The whole book is filled with spells and things. If the book is to be believed, she is the mother of witches. I thought they didn't exist. They were legends of women with the sort of magic that could create or destroy, obviously a myth or they would have used them against us instead of sending a single monster,

But what if, what if I tried the spell on the last page? The one to speak with our Goddess? What if I could talk to her outside of my dreams? I have to try it. I need to know why she is in my dreams. If there is some way to fix all the damage I have done by coming here. If there are answers to be found anywhere, I just know she will have them. My door opens and I close the book quickly, turning I see Epaphras looking at me like I am behaving oddly. I suppose standing in the middle of my room reading a book is odd.

"Is it dinnertime already?"

His eyes narrow as he studies me. "It is. What book is that you have?"

My cheeks heat and for once I am grateful as I lie to him, "It's a romance novel. A lot more racy than I thought it would be."

His lips twist. "Oh, you read those? I always heard they were for the less intelligent."

My jaw drops. No, he did not. "Are you saying I'm stupid or less intelligent for reading romance?"

His eyes widen, and he backs up a step. "That is not what I meant at all. Dinner! Yes, it is time for dinner! You should get dressed. The guards and I will escort you to the dining room and the kings will meet us there."

"Fine. But you can go wait outside for me. I will be ready in a few, and I will choose my own outfit."

He grumbles on his way out the door and as soon as it

closes behind him; I look for a place to hide the book. Not the closet. He is in there more than I am. The bed is no good. The kings pay way too much attention to it. My gaze travels across the room and stops at the window. More of an arrow slit, really, but curtained to look like a real window. The curtains drape all the way to the floor. I dash over and gently pull a curtain just far enough away from the wall that I can slip the book behind it. I am careful to smooth it back into place and it is perfect. No one will notice it there.

That done, I run into the closet and shuck the pants and shirt I was wearing in favor of a long skirt with a split up one side and a fitted top. Both have a pretty opalescent sheen to them and I feel like they set off my skin nicely. Grabbing a pair of shoes, I head for the bathroom, where I set them on the counter. My hair gets shoved into a loose twist at the back. I think about makeup, but I am not feeling like doing the whole thing, so I just refresh it. It really kind of works better with the outfit, anyway.

Slipping on my shoes, I head for the door with one last longing glance at the curtain hiding my book.

* * *

Dinner drags on forever. I really love spending time with them, but I feel like I need to do this now. Like there is a clock somewhere ticking away the time I have left to do it.

When dinner is over, I let them walk me to my room, but instead of letting them in, I tell them I need a night to sleep on things, without the distraction of them.

Knox grins at me. "Distraction? Hmm, I suppose we don't want you over worked. Sleep well, darling. Call out if you need us."

Malic put his hands on my arms, rubbing them with his thumbs. "Are you all right? I know the attacks must have been a lot. Don't brood on them, it just closes you off and makes you a sour jackass."

I laugh, "No. I am good. I just need a night to myself. I am not used to so much attention. It is strange and I need to be alone with me for a bit."

He nods, "If that is all it is," he looks at me like he doesn't really believe me, "then I wish you a good night alone. In your room. Where you will be the entire night, correct?"

"Where else would I sleep?"

He snatches me up and kisses me hard. Setting me down, he says, "See that you do."

I turn and open the door to my room, entering and closing the door behind me. I walk to the bathroom and clean up like I am getting ready for bed. That takes long enough that I am quite sure they have gone to their own beds by now. Stepping softly, I make my way to the curtain that hides my book. I am afraid it won't be there as I pull the curtain back. But there it is, safe and waiting. Picking it up, I straighten and flip it open to the last page. Reading over the ritual again reassures me. Some candles, a clear picture in my mind of her, and her name.

Setting the book on the bed, I go to the door and quietly pull the rug over to black the light from being seen under the door. Back through the room to collect five candles. I am certain these candles were probably not meant to be used, but I don't care. I need to do this and I am not asking for different ones. They'll have too many questions and with how protective they are over me, no way am I telling them what I plan to do.

I am trying to go faster as the need to do this presses in on me. My heart is racing. I keep referring to the book for every little thing. It's like I have lost my ability to retain information. I finally get it all set up, and I bring the book into the middle of the candles with me. A strike of the match and shortly all five candles are lit. One last glance at the book. Deep breath, probably nothing will happen, right?

Holding her image in my mind, I whisper, "Hekate." A chill breeze wraps itself around me and my eyes fly open to see her there before me. Holy fuck, it worked. It worked. My eyes round as everything I wanted to say to her is gone, and I am left with an overwhelming sense of coming home. Tears scorch their way down my face as I fall to my knees before her, overcome with emotion.

Her hands are cool and comforting as she lifts me from the floor like I weigh nothing. "Come, stand up. There, there, little one. I know it is hard not fitting in, but you were meant to stand out from the rest. You are the key to it all. I have been waiting centuries for this very moment when I get to meet you."

That one sentence stopped me. "What? Why? I'm nobody, nothing. Why would you have been waiting for me?"

And that's when she slapped me. My head rocked back. She held me steady and waited till I looked back at her, rubbing my still smarting face. Her eyes are narrowed and her jaw set as she says, "You are the result of so much work and effort and love, it took so much to bring things together to ensure that you happened, that you are as you are right this minute. I will not ever allow you to say that you are nothing! You are everything! All of our hopes for the future rest on you. You are the key to it all. Never again do I want to hear you describe yourself as nothing. Do you understand me?"

Swallowing, I nod. "I think you may have gotten the point across."

She nods, "Good. Now come sit. There is much you need to know and not terribly long before Malic tries to sneak in and reassure himself that you are, in fact, within these walls. I would take you elsewhere, but he might explode with concern when he found the room empty. Or turn my big island into rubble."

A giggle bubbles up and out at her wry tone. "I suppose he might at that."

She nods and the sting from the slap fades away like it never was as we sit on the small couch. "Before I tell you what I feel you need to know, what questions have you got for me?"

"Are the attacks my fault?"

"Yes, and no. They have to happen."

"Will there be another?"

She smiles, "Ah, now there is a good question. Yes."

"Will I be able to save them both? Will I know beforehand so that I can warn everyone?"

"Maybe. That depends on you and how well you take to your lessons."

"Lessons? Are you going to tell me what lessons to take to ensure that I can?"

She nods, "I am. One more question, then I must tell you what I came here to say. Our time will be gone before you know it."

"I felt like I needed to keep this secret from them. Will I need to continue to keep it a secret from them? Oh, I know it's a second question, but will I still see you in my dreams?"

She laughs. "I will grant it. No, you don't, you should definitely tell them. And yes, you will."

"Oh, thank goodness. I don't want to keep things from them."

"Indeed. Now, you are the first of the witches to awaken. Summoning me has unlocked your power. You will need to work to control it and it will not be easy. There is no easy road with magic. Especially not for the first. The heart and mind are both needed for proper control of your magic. One without the other, disaster.

You must gain control before it is fully unleashed. Right now, it is similar to a water line that has long been blocked with the seal freshly ripped off. It is a trickle. Little tiny streams starting to ease out. All too soon, though, the dam will burst and there will be a flood. You must be ready when that happens. At best, you have a week. If you get terribly stressed, well, that may rip it wide open right then."

"Holy shit, I am just a bomb waiting to explode."

"In a manner of speaking, yes. But you hold the power to control it. You will be the strongest of my witches. You read the history, yes?"

Nodding, I say, "Yes, is it all true? Did they really slaughter so many? For power that was never meant for them?"

"They did. And they are back. As is their deity. He has operatives here on my land, working to overthrow the kings and take control of you."

"Oh shit, it's them? Eirene is one of them? My step-mother? And Ingemar?"

"They are part of it, yes. Now, you are the only one that knows my name right now. You may tell anyone inside this castle right now, none that come later with the exception of the other kings. When you tell them, every-one, not just the kings, it will unlock things inside them. Not magic. Only a very few will have that." She smiles. "One of them is your mother. Your real mother, not Eirene. Her magic will seem small but at the right time their might will be revealed. She will be able to visit the bookshelf where you found my book, and you will need to go back there for the others that will be there waiting. That shelf of books is solely for the two of you. Everyone else has their own books waiting to be found. Do not leave them out, while no one here will see them. I cannot promise that he won't have his people looking for them. It would be very bad for them to have any of the books."

"Ok. Keep your name inside the castle, only people here now. Books just for Dagma and I. All the kings get to hear your name, whether or not they are here. Guard the books. Do I have it all, the basics?"

"Control your magic. Put out your hand," she says and I do. Palm up, I hold it out in the air before me. She says, "Focus on a fire in the palm of your hand."

I look at my hand, picturing a candle flame there in my palm. When it pops into being, my eyes widen and my breath catches. I look to Hekate, "I did it!" The grin on my face comes straight from my heart.

She smiles and her eyes glitter brightly, "Yes, you did. Now let go of the image and close your hand."

I do as she says, and the flame disappears, but I am ecstatic. I want to jump for joy, but there is a whole Goddess sitting here with me, so I opt for restraint.

She looks toward the door and then back at me. "Malic will be here in moments. You did very well and I am so proud of you. I will see you in your dreams, though I cannot visit you in person for some time. Remember all I said here and you will not fail me, first in my line of witches. Whatever happens, you remember that you are descended directly from me and you are so very loved." She places her hands on either side of my face and draws me forward, placing a kiss on my forehead. As I straighten, she looks toward the door. Turning back, she says, "There he is. I will visit you soon."

Her form fades away as Malic quietly opens the door. His face is a picture of surprise when he sees me sitting here, looking directly at him. I smile, "Go get Knox. He should hear this too."

Twenty-Two

INGEMAR

It is unfortunate that we need her to go along with this, but none of us could see any way around it. It will strengthen our case so much more to have her there attesting to how we all protected her from the kings. My car pulls up in front of her home and I get out when my man opens the door for me. Just looking up at the place for a moment, my mind awash with memories of Conrí. He was too good for this world. It was no surprise when I heard he died attacked out on the road. He probably offered to help them kill him because he thought they would be better off for it.

Straightening my jacket, I head for the door. They show me in to Eirene's office immediately. Of course, she is not in here and I sit down to wait. If today is like every time before, it will be a solid twenty minutes before she arrives.

Sure enough, twenty minutes on the dot, Eirene walks in. She is insufferable in so many ways. Her attitude and bearing as a woman, just ridiculous. Widow or not, she should defer. This thing that helps her, it's given her ideas above her station in life. I hope I get to watch as she dies. Even her manner of dress, a woman her age, should not be showing off her body with form fitting attire such as hers. Though it is nice to look at. She moves slowly as she seats herself. A petty game, but I've employed the same tactics myself.

"Ingemar, I wish I could say it was good to see you, but the recent failure is quite troubling."

I barely stop my eyes from rolling. "It is. Very troubling. And that is precisely why I am here."

She raises a brow at me like I am a child with what is likely a not well thought out idea. Her death is going to be a glorious day indeed. "Do tell Ingemar I am curious as to how you intend to fix this."

Gripping the arms of the chair I tell her, "The other lords and myself were thinking," about watching as you roast over an open fire, "that we should spin it differently than it actually happened. We want to hold another rally. During which we will appear quite battered. We will announce to everyone that we went to the castle with you, the other lords joining with us in a show of solidarity, to try to convince them to release Valdís. The king was greatly angered that we would ask for his toy back and attacked us all. We all encircled you to protect you, you being a lady and it being our duty to protect you. Barely making it out of the castle with our lives and poor Valdís still trapped inside with that monster."

Her hands are steepled in front of her as she mulls over what I said. I can't imagine what there is to think about. It's the best idea possible with what we have to work with. Finally she says, "Yes, I think that will work, with one change. The king is powerful and supposed to be a monster. It cannot be only you all that are bruised. I will ensure that I too am bruised because the king hit me at least once as we tried to escape."

I am shocked that she suggested that. We thought about it but never dreamed that she would be willing. "Yes, perfect. We didn't want to put you in that position, but that would make it better."

"Yes, I know. When do you plan to hold this rally?"

"In the morning, early."

"Excellent. Get yourselves beat up immediately so the bruises have the maximum amount of time to coalesce. I will do the same."

"Wonderful. Will you ride with me to the rally tomorrow morning?"

"I will. I believe it will seem more believable if I prefer to be surrounded by my protectors than if I arrive alone."

"Then I bid you good day and I will see you shortly after seven in the morning."

Valdís

As I wait for Malic and Knox to return, I am still a lot overwhelmed with it all. I have to put on a good act for them, but what the fuck is happening here? The Goddess of our people, the one who wiped her name from everywhere, gave me her name and tells me I am loved? I am the work of centuries? What?

She also slapped me, but I guess not many other people can say they were slapped by an actual goddess and lived. I have to wonder, what happens if I fail? That train wreck of thought is stopped by Malic and a very displeased Knox walking in. Knox is wearing what appears to be the blanket from his bed as he comes to sit in the spot so recently vacated by Hekate. He relaxes into the cushions before his nose twitches and he bolts upright. "What is that scent? Who was here? That smell isn't you. Who was here? I don't recognize that scent. Are they still here?" He is peering around my room even as Malic starts checking the place. I can't help myself. I start to laugh. Knox looks down at me. "Why are you laughing?"

Malic narrows his eyes at me and walks over, his search abandoned. Still giggling, I manage to tell them, "There was someone here, but it isn't anyone that you could defend me from. If she had wanted me dead, it would have been done before Malic decided to come check on whether or not I stayed in my room."

Knox is not terribly awake and doesn't quite catch on, but Malic's eyes go round and he says, "SHE was here?"

I nod, "In the flesh."

He snatches the chair closer to the small couch I am still seated on while Knox readjusts his blanket and grumbles about not being awake enough for this shit. He seats himself and looks toward me, but Malic speaks first. "Why was she here? It isn't good, is it?"

"Well, no. It really isn't. So I went to the library today and found a book that had her name in it as well as a ritual to call her. So I did it."

Malic interjects, "We'll talk about why we didn't know you were out of your room later. What happened after you performed the ritual?"

Shrugging, I tell him, "She was there. Between one breath and the next, she was before me. She said I am the key and that I should share her name with you all. That it would unlock things." I watch them closely as I say, "Hekate."

They freeze, not so much as a breath of air between them. Malic's eyes tear up. "She showed me a vision of you once. It was right before she locked everything away. When I asked her why she would show me what I longed for most in this world, she said that my soul would need something to hold onto, even if I didn't consciously remember it."

Knox has buried his face in my lap as Malic spoke, holding to me like I am his tether to the planet. After Malic has been silent a moment, he says something into my lap. "We can't hear you, Knox. Take your mouth off my thighs if you want to talk."

He turns his head to the side facing Malic, "She told me I would have an open heart and be widely regarded as the kindest of the kings when you appeared, for all that I would viciously torture anyone trying to harm the people of this land. She told me that the library was always for you, no matter how much I loved it. And that when you arrived, that was the sign that the Outsiders were making a move again. That we would be called to protect her daughters."

Malic nods. "I'm going to check on our brothers and see if I can't get them to hurry it up already. Things are going to get real bad real quick once people find out what you are, and I need a little more explanation on that. Most think they are Hekate's children, even if they don't know her name. If you are descended directly from her, does that give you special powers?"

Focusing on a shelf across the room, I tell them, "If I understand correctly, it means I am a witch. The first of my kind to wake up." Licking my lips, I look over at Malic. Knox didn't tense, but I can't see his face either way.

Malic is steady, not a trace of upset as he says, "Do you know the history of the witches? What happened to all of them?"

I nod. "It was in the book. I do have questions though, if you could maybe answer them? Or try?" He and Knox both nod. "Why? I think the book said it was about power. Is that true? Did they slaughter all the witches for power?"

Malic nods, "They did. Did the book tell you that only women are or can be witches?"

"Oh sweet goddess, they murdered women for having a power they couldn't have?"

He nods, "They did. It was blocked from our memories till now but, even here. It happened at the same time as the assassinations of our brothers. We were not capable of coping well with it, so we sent away as many of the outsiders as we could get rounded up. To most of them, we are a myth. Our island sank into the sea centuries ago and they can find no proof that we existed at all."

"So they exterminated us. Killed us for being more than they could be. And Hekate hid whoever remained, making sure that we thought witches had been eradicated so we would be safe. Until now... She said there would be others. What do you think the likelihood is that they will be attacked for power everywhere again?"

Knox lifts his head, a frown twisting his face. "It is nearly guaranteed. Especially since they are already moving against us. There is no way they will allow the women with power to live. It is probable that they will work to use them against us if at all possible."

"We can't leave them there."

Malic tips his head to one side. "We can't seek out every witch on the planet waking up and protect them. It isn't possible."

"I will find a way. This isn't negotiable or something that can be ignored Knox. These women are effectively my sisters. I may not know them yet, but that doesn't change the fact that their lives are in danger the minute their magic begins to emerge. Not only that, but every witch that can be caught and pressed into service by the outsiders is a threat to us. This is dual purposed. I have to learn more..." I look at the door, longing to go to the library now and grab some more books, knowing they are going to insist I need sleep at some point. "I am not even the only witch here in the castle right now."

Knox sits up. "What do you mean, you aren't the only one?"

"I mean, my mother, my birth mother, is also a witch. Hekate told me."

Malic nods. "It used to run in families like that. It makes sense she would want your mother to share in that with you. For tonight, you need to sleep. I see you looking at the door. You are not visiting the library tonight. Visit tomorrow with Dagma."

Knox says, "Now that you are done casting spells to call Hekate, can we sleep in here with you? I don't want to go back to my lonely bed."

"Yes, you both can definitely stay here with me." Just

like that, Knox stands, his blanket forgotten on the couch. He leans over and scoops me up, a few strides and he is sliding into the bed with me tucked securely in front of him. Malic turns off the lights and is quickly in bed with us. Sleep overtakes me before I can protest that I need to do things.

Rhiannon writes steamy paranormal romance. She is an avid reader of many authors in a variety of genre though she tends more toward paranormal.

She has three former pound puppies that she dotes on and three daughters that she adores.

Rhiannon has lived in multiple states though she is currently residing in North Carolina. Wandering, witching, and reading with her puppies and husband are what she does when she isn't writing.

To learn about what is happening in Rhiannon's world and get loads of pupper cuteness, sign up for the by using the QR code below to visit my website.

Mercy of the Vampire King

Shame of the Vampire King

Pursuit of the Vampire King

Prey of the Vampire King

Reign of the Vampire King

Coming Soon

Love and Vampires Series

Olivia's Fall

Olivia's Prison

Olivia's Flight

Olivia's Family

Warriors of the Old Gods

A Dream of Blood

A Dream of Wolves

A Dream of Stone

A Dream of Ravens

A Dream of Bones